PRAISE FOR *Always Emily*:

A Junior Library Guild selection

A Parents' Choice Awards Recommended Seal

★ "Filled with life, death, mystery and witty humor."—*School Library Journal,* starred review

★ "MacColl has crafted a fictional tale of suspense and romance that is guaranteed to bring new readership to MacColl, as well as to the classic tales by both Brontë sisters." —*VOYA (Voice of Youth Advocates),* starred review

"Equal parts gothic melodrama and Nancy Drew derring-do." —*Kirkus Reviews*

"A well-paced period mystery with just the right dash of romance." —*Publishers Weekly*

PRAISE FOR *Nobody's Secret*:

A Bank Street College of Education Best Book of the Year

★ "A well-crafted page-turner. . . . MacColl once again brings a strong female protagonist to life." —*School Library Journal,* starred review

★ "Intriguing. . . . MacColl skillfully draws from Dickenson's life to create a vision of the young poet as sharp-thinking, nature-obsessed, and determinedly curious." —*Publishers Weekly,* starred review

★ "Suspenseful, often humorous." —Shelf Awareness for Readers, starred review

"Plenty of intrigue and suspense. . . . A highly imaginative and sensitive heroine in the tradition of Jo March and Anne Shirley." —*The Bulletin of the Center for Children's Books*

PRAISE FOR *Prisoners in the Palace*:

A Junior Library Guild selection

A Kids' Indie Next List selection

★ "A great read." —*School Library Journal,* starred review

"A whip-smart, spunky protagonist and a worthy heroine to root for." —*Publishers Weekly*

"Fascinating." —*Horn Book Guide*

Always EMILY

Also by Michaela MacColl:

The Revelation of Louisa May

Nobody's Secret

Promise the Night

Prisoners in the Palace

Always

EMILY

A NOVEL OF INTRIGUE AND ROMANCE BY

MICHAELA MacColl

CHRONICLE BOOKS

SAN FRANCISCO

First Chronicle Books LLC paperback edition, published in 2015.
Originally published in hardcover in 2014 by Chronicle Books LLC.

ISBN 978-1-4521-4130-5

The Library of Congress has cataloged the original edition as follows:

MacColl, Michaela, author.
  Always Emily : a novel of intrigue and romance / by Michaela MacColl.
    pages cm
  Summary: Young Emily and Charlotte Brontë solve a mystery.
  ISBN 978-1-4521-1174-2 (alk. paper)
  1. Brontë, Emily, 1818–1848—Juvenile fiction. 2. Brontë, Charlotte, 1816–1855—Juvenile fiction. 3. Women authors, English—19th century—Juvenile fiction. 4. Detective and mystery stories. 5. Great Britain—History—1800–1837—Juvenile fiction. [1. Mystery and detective stories. 2. Brontë, Emily, 1818–1848—Fiction. 3. Brontë, Charlotte, 1816–1855—Fiction. 4. Women authors—Fiction. 5. Great Britain—History—1800–1837—Fiction.] I. Title.

PZ7.M13384Alw 2014
813.6--dc23

                    2013019086

Manufactured in China.

Design by Kate Cunningham and Sara Gillingham Studio.
Cover design by Kate Cunningham.
Typeset in Hoefler Text, Copperplate, and Shelley Allegro.

10 9 8 7 6 5 4 3 2 1

Chronicle Books LLC
680 Second Street
San Francisco, CA 94107

Chronicle Books—we see things differently. Become part of our community at www.chroniclebooks.com/teen.

For Margaux. Always challenging.
Always worth it. I love you. —Mom

I got the sexton, who was digging Linton's grave, to
remove the earth off her coffin lid, and I opened it.
I thought, once, I would have stayed there: when I
saw her face again—it is hers yet!

CHURCH OF HAWORTH, HAWORTH, ENGLAND

May 1825

The minister pronounced the final benediction for
Elizabeth Brontë, aged ten. The funeral was finally over.

The surviving Brontës huddled in the family pew.
Charlotte, the eldest child at nine, sat stiffly, her back perfectly straight. She frowned at her younger sister, Emily, who
had fidgeted unconscionably during the long service. Then
she clutched her eight-year-old brother Branwell's hand. With
a loud sniff, he snatched it away and wiped his nose with his
knuckles.

The sexton led the Reverend Brontë and the children to a wide gravestone embedded in the church floor. Their mother and other sister, Marie, were buried beneath it and now Elizabeth would join them.

As the Elizabeth-size coffin was brought down from the altar, a sob escaped from Charlotte. Emily stood off to one side, her chin up despite the tears rolling down her cheeks. Branwell blew his nose hard and pressed his body against his father's side.

The sexton, an old family friend, levered up the stone slab, exposing a crypt beneath the floor. When he placed a ladder inside the crypt, a heavy, foul dust floated up and obscured their vision. Charlotte and Branwell gagged.

Emily stepped forward, her color high and her eyes shining. "I see her," she whispered. "The shape of dear Elizabeth." Holding her hands out, she stepped to the edge of the crypt.

"Emily!" Charlotte yanked her back from the precipice.

"Don't fall in," Branwell cried. "Then I'll have hardly any sisters at all."

The sexton climbed inside the crypt. His assistant easily handed down the tiny coffin as though it were no weight at all.

"Thank you, John," Rev. Brontë said in a heavy voice when the sexton rejoined them.

"My sympathies, reverend." He nodded to the children and added, "Do you have any other tasks for me before I close up the crypt?"

"Yes," Rev. Brontë said, drawing him to the vestry.

The children were left alone. Branwell moved a safe distance away from the opening to stand with his back to a stone column. His complexion had a greenish hue. Charlotte was about to join him when Emily broke the silence.

"Mr. Brown is going to seal up the grave?"

Branwell frowned. "Well, he won't leave a big open hole in the floor."

"But how will Elizabeth ascend if she's locked in that hole?"

"A person's spirit can ascend through anything," Charlotte declared.

"Through stone? Are you certain?" Emily persisted. "Have you ever seen a soul go to heaven?"

"No one can see it, Emily," Charlotte said. "The ascension is invisible."

"In paintings we see the angel flying upward," Emily retorted. She might be only seven years old, but she was confident her logic was irrefutable.

"Don't be stupid, Emily." Branwell finally roused himself from his misery. "That's just in art. Not life."

"How do you know?" Emily shot back. "Just because you and Charlotte are older than me doesn't mean you know everything. What if Elizabeth can't escape unless the crypt is open?"

"Don't be morbid, Emily," Charlotte scolded. "The crypt won't be opened until another one of us dies."

"Exactly! So let's release her now." Emily placed her foot on the topmost rung of the ladder.

"Don't do it, Emily!" cried Branwell.

Charlotte balked, glancing sharply between their father speaking in hushed tones with his sexton and her sister descending into the crypt.

"Come on, Charlotte," Emily said. "Don't you want to know what it's like down there?"

Charlotte hesitated, then snatched a candle from the altar and followed Emily down to the narrow space. It was damp and smelt of decay. Built-in stone alcoves held the coffins on either side of her. Elizabeth's coffin was on a bottom shelf.

"There aren't any latches," Emily whispered, running the tips of her fingers across the side of the coffin.

"There's no need."

Emily reached toward Elizabeth's coffin to lift open the lid.

"Emily! You go too far!" Charlotte dropped the candle and grabbed Emily's wrists so tightly that Emily cried out.

"What harm can it do to look?" Emily pried Charlotte's fingers away from her hand. "If I'm right, her soul can soar away. If I'm wrong, at least we can wish her a proper farewell."

Charlotte eyes shot back and forth between the coffin and her sister. Finally she said, "I'll do it. You're too little."

Emily stepped back. Charlotte lifted the lid, her mouth twisting to keep from gagging on the sickly smell. Aghast, she let the lid drop.

"Open it, Charlotte! I want to see her dear countenance!" Emily's face was distorted and grotesque in the flickering candlelight.

"What if it isn't our sister anymore?" Charlotte asked urgently. "What if she's become something horrible?"

The thought gave even Emily pause. After a silence, she said, "I don't care!" She lunged toward the coffin and threw open the lid.

The sisters stared at the still body of ten-year-old Elizabeth. Her face was sunken from the ravages of the graveyard cough that had killed her. Her pretty hair had been cut short at the boarding school by a headmaster who thought long hair encouraged vanity. Her skin was pale, like ivory.

"She looks at peace," Charlotte said, relieved.

"She does, doesn't she?" Emily said, staring intently at her dead sister's face. She reached over and brushed a lock of hair from Elizabeth's cold forehead. "Do you think we've released her soul?"

Before Charlotte could answer, they were startled by a booming voice above their heads. "Charlotte! Get out of there now!" Their father peered down at them, holding Branwell's hand. He was angrier than they had ever heard him before. "And you brought Emily with you? For shame!"

Emily started to speak, but Charlotte put her fingers to her lips. It would do no good for both of them to be punished.

Charlotte climbed out, followed by Emily. Standing in front of their father, they didn't dare meet his eyes. After an excruciating moment, he said, "Charlotte, what were you thinking? You must be more responsible. Don't you realize you're the oldest now?" His voice trembled and tears ran down his cheeks.

Charlotte put her hands to her face and sobbed.

Emily put her arm around Charlotte's shoulders. She couldn't imagine anything more awful than being the responsible one.

Many [girls], already smitten, went home
only to die: some died at the school, and were
buried quietly and quickly, the nature of
the malady forbidding delay.

CHAPTER ONE

August 1835

"How much farther?" Emily asked. Her long body pressed into the corner of the carriage seat, as if she were trying to propel herself back home toward Haworth.

"A mile less than the last time you asked," Charlotte said between gritted teeth. She sat primly in the corner, her feet barely touching the floor. Charlotte tried to make up for her lack of inches with perfect posture. A notebook and pen were at hand, but Charlotte hadn't written a single word. Emily had proved to be a distraction as a traveling companion.

"You didn't tell me this school was so far away," Emily said, staring out the dirty window. "I never would have agreed to go."

"You didn't agree," Charlotte pointed out. "Father insisted."

"Because you badgered him without respite."

"Badger?" Charlotte's hand went to her bodice. "I'm sorry if planning for the future is bothersome to you and Father."

Emily glared at her sister with raised eyebrows. Suddenly she tugged the window open and stuck her head out.

"Em, close the window. Ladies don't thrust their heads out into the road. It's common."

"I don't care what anyone thinks." Emily shoved her body farther out the window. She recognized the landscape—they were near the great bog of Crow Hill. Charlotte had lied when she said they were making progress; they were barely ten miles from home. The landscape was still familiar. The great green hills were just starting to turn purple with the heather. In September, these hills would be heavy with the scent of the flowers and their vibrant color would swamp the eyes. But Emily wouldn't be there to see it.

On the horizon, beneath a row of fir trees stunted by the constant wind on the moors, Emily noticed a figure on horseback galloping across the top of a hill, the perfect symbol of the liberty she was giving up. Emily wanted to fix the memory of that rider in her mind. When she was locked up at school this anonymous figure would be her talisman; a promise that someday Emily would roam the moors again.

Suddenly her shoulder was gripped by a small hand and
Emily was hauled inside. Charlotte, stumbling against the
motion of the carriage, slammed the window shut. "The moors
will still be there when you get home." She sat back down and
crossed her arms.

"But how long will that be?" Emily said. "When you went
to school, you stayed for two entire years."

"I came home for holidays." She patted Emily's leg. "And
you will, too. You'll be home for Christmas."

"Four months!" Emily's voice was high and anxious. "How
will I stand it?"

"I've told you time and time again—school is not a punishment. Father is a fine teacher, but at Roe Head School I
learned things I never could have at the parsonage."

Emily's expression spoke eloquently of her doubts.

"Don't scowl at me like that, Emily. I've learned languages
and geography and grammar. Your education has been too
eccentric. If you're to earn a living, you must know the academic
subjects as well as music, deportment, and the rest." Charlotte's
words slipped glibly off her tongue from long repetition.

"I don't care about earning my living," Emily exclaimed.
"No one wants me to work except you!"

"Look at me, Emily," Charlotte commanded. When
Emily continued to stare out the window, Charlotte reached
over and grabbed her sister's chin. "You're seventeen now,
and we must face the facts of our situation. Father is our only

bulwark against destitution. When he dies, we lose our income and our home. We must be prepared to support ourselves."

Emily batted Charlotte's hand away. "Your concern for the future keeps you imprisoned in the present. Why lock yourself up in a school when Father's healthy as an ox? You worry for nothing."

Charlotte's hand clenched and unclenched. "How can you forget his illness this past spring? We might have lost him then!" Her wide brown eyes filled with tears as she remembered those days nursing their father. It was then she'd formulated a plan to save the family. She would return to school, but as a teacher. Rather than a full salary, her recompense would include tuition for Emily. It was the perfect plan. Except for one thing. Emily.

"I have no interest in teaching or governessing." Emily spoke with deliberation. Charlotte had tried to arrange everything without consulting Emily, who would not soon forgive her sister for it.

"Would you prefer marriage?" Charlotte asked. "Because that's your only alternative." A snort was Emily's only response. Charlotte leaned back against the dusty cushion and closed her eyes. Melodrama was exhausting.

After another mile or so, Emily spoke in a softer voice. "What is this school like? Will I hate it?"

Charlotte opened her eyes and smiled. "You may like it very much. I made good friends there. You've met my friend Ellen. She's lovely, don't you agree?"

Emily tugged at the fingers of her darned gloves, picking at the ragged seams. "I suppose so."

"The days are filled with learning," Charlotte continued. "It's very well organized."

Emily's eyes filled with malice; she asked, "And how much writing did you do while you were there? Did the Adventures of Angria continue at Roe Head or did they shrivel wasted on the vine?"

Charlotte was silent.

"I seem to remember you writing frantically when you came home," Emily said.

"Miss Wooler, the headmistress, says we must bend our inclination to our duty. If necessary, I'll sacrifice my writing to earn security for my family," Charlotte muttered.

"Selflessness is your specialty, not mine," Emily retorted. "What if I am not willing to surrender my dreams?"

Charlotte glared at Emily, who had the grace to look abashed.

With her facility for logic that alternately impressed and infuriated Charlotte, Emily leapt to another argument. "If I have to go to school, why do I have to change the way I look?" Emily ran her fingers across her scalp and bits of crimped hair broke off in her hands. "Look what your hairdressing did! I look absurd with curls."

Charlotte privately agreed Emily's fair coloring and light eyes were better suited to a less labored hairdressing, but she hastened to reassure her sister. "No, it's fashionable." She wrapped one of her dark ringlets around her finger. "I'm trying to spare you the mistakes I made. When I arrived at school, everyone made fun of my clothes and hair."

"What do I care about what people think?" Emily snapped her fingers with a loud snap, a habit Charlotte deplored because she couldn't do it.

"You're not in Haworth anymore," Charlotte said. "I'm trying to keep you from being lonely like I was at first."

Emily shot a glance at her sister. With an unfamiliar pang of guilt, she reached out and took Charlotte's hand. "You're trying to help me and I'm acting the shrew." After a moment, she added, "I'm out of my element and it's putting me out of sorts. Tell me more about the school so I know what to expect."

"The students take long walks, weather permitting. You'll like that."

"Weather permitting? I walk in any weather. The more wuthering the better." Stormy weather on the moors was called a wuthering and it was one of Emily's favorite words.

"We walk often enough," Charlotte said firmly. "Miss Wooler says it builds strong bodies and spurs the appetite. The food is quite good—and unlike home, we don't have to do the washing up."

Emily looked sidelong at Charlotte. "It's not like . . . Cowan Bridge?" This was the question she had avoided asking ever since school had become inevitable. Two of their sisters had died at Cowan Bridge from cold and neglect.

"Of course not!" Charlotte contemplated her sister with pity. No wonder Emily was so obstinate about school; how could she have not seen it? "Cowan Bridge was an awful place. Father would never make that mistake again." Her voice contained a speck of blame for their father's carelessness. "And I'll be there with you. There's nothing to fear."

"You and I will share a room, won't we?" Emily asked.

Charlotte had dreaded this question. "You hate sharing a room with me!"

"But it would be a familiar irritation," Emily said.

"I'm to be a teacher, so I'll have my own room," Charlotte said, looking at Emily warily. "You'll be in the dormitory."

Emily straightened up and glared at Charlotte. "I have to share a room with strangers?"

Charlotte took a deep breath and delivered the worst news. "You'll share a bed with another student."

Emily's face was like stone.

"But in the winter, it's handy for the warmth," Charlotte hurried on. "And it's fun to have someone to whisper secrets with in the dark."

"My secrets are my own," Emily said flatly.

The carriage slowed and turned onto a gravel drive. Emily abandoned Charlotte and studied the school as the carriage crunched up the incline. The building was large—three stories—and surrounded by giant oak and cedar trees.

"You didn't say it was so big," Emily whispered.

"Truly, Emily, it's a good school," Charlotte answered. "You could be happy here. If only you'll try."

The carriage shuddered to a stop. The driver hopped down from his perch atop the roof and opened the door. Charlotte, stiff from the ride, awkwardly climbed down. Emily jumped to the ground without using the step.

Staring up at the imposing wooden doors, Emily muttered, "I won't last a week."

"Nonsense," Charlotte said, her cheerful tone ringing ominously false. "Give it a month. By then you will have settled in and you won't want to be anywhere else."

As if they had a heft and weight, Emily pushed away her fears with a wave of her hand. "A month then, Charlotte." But in the privacy of her mind, Emily added, "After then, with or without you, I'm going home."

How few would believe that from sources purely

imaginary such happiness could be derived.

CHAPTER TWO

*C*harlotte closed her eyes and imagined the next scene in her story.

> *The queen wore a velvet dress of emerald green, set-*
> *ting off her golden tresses. A breeze lifted her standard and*
> *the bold silk snapped in the wind. She rode at the head of*
> *an enormous army, but her duty meant nothing to her. The*
> *duke was coming.*
> *A neigh drew her eyes to the top of the small hill, under*
> *the ancient oak tree. The duke of Zamorna appeared, seated*
> *expertly on his horse of war. She caught her breath and urged*

her own mare forward. Her breath grew faster and shallower. Her body felt disconnected from the earth and she knew if he only asked it, she could fly away. But his face was impassive, his nostrils flaring, and his supple lips pressed tightly together. Had he forgiven her?

"Your Grace," she whispered.

In a swift, agile movement, he dismounted. Without a word, he held out his arms. Heedless of her royal dignity, she fell into his embrace. The beating of his heart dominated her own.

"So this is heaven," she thought. Or said aloud. It mattered not anymore.

His voice rough with passion, he said, "Dear heart. . . ."

"Miss Brontë?" A hand touched Charlotte's arm.

Charlotte started. Her breath came quick and short. For a moment, she was suspended between two worlds: Angria, the imagined land of handsome dukes and passionate queens, and the tedium of her life at Roe Head School. She had to blink to see the classroom clearly. Her students, half a dozen young ladies ranging from the age of eleven to sixteen, stared at her curiously. Angria retreated back into her imagination with the inexorability of the tide.

"Miss Brontë? I asked you twice to check my answers." The simpering girl in front of her was typical of all her students: middle class, of limited intellect, and utterly dull. This student was always the first to finish her work—an assignment Charlotte had carefully planned with the hope of occupying the girls for the remainder of the class.

"Give it to me, Miss Lister," Charlotte said, recovering herself. Holding the paper to her nose, the only way Charlotte's weak eyes could make out the cramped handwriting, she scanned the composition. The girls exchanged glances and tittered as they always did. "Sit down and rewrite the conclusion. Haste is wasteful if you cannot write to good effect."

With a sullen expression on her face, Miss Lister tilted her head and asked loudly, "Miss Brontë, are you feeling ill? You look flushed."

"Don't be impertinent," Charlotte retorted. "I assure you I am perfectly well." She caught a glimpse of the clock. Half an hour remained before tea. She pulled out her grading ledger and inserted a clean piece of paper over her neat columns of her students' scores.

Tilting the ledger so her students couldn't see what she was doing, she dipped her pen in the ink and began to write. The story flowed onto the paper as easily as rain falling to the earth. Only when she reached the moment when the duke declared his love did her hand falter. Desperately, she tried to imagine what he would have said if he had not been interrupted. Oh, the tiresome Miss Lister! Because of her ill-timed interference, Charlotte might never be able to re-create that moment of passionate bliss.

The clock struck four o'clock and with relief she dismissed the class with a clap of her hands.

As soon as they were gone, Charlotte retreated upstairs to her tiny dormitory room. As a teacher, she had the small luxury of sharing neither her room nor a bed, a fact Emily still resented. But this precious solitude was the only thing making Roe Head bearable.

Sitting at the rickety table that served as her desk, she pulled out her story and tried to write the ending again. But the romance was gone. Instead of the heat of the duke's embrace, Charlotte felt a cold emptiness. The loss was overwhelming. She pushed the paper aside and massaged her skull with her fingers, loosening her dark hair from her tight bun.

"What am I going to do?" she whispered. Writing about the duke brought an unseemly warmth to her cheeks and an ache deep inside herself. Her writing, her infernal internal world, was a temptation she should not, must not succumb to. She must put aside the duke and return to her duty. Her future was not to be a great literary light. She was doomed to teach other people's children until she grew old and withered. "But must I sit from day to day, chained to this dreary life, missing any chance for love and adventure?"

Tap, tap.

Charlotte tried to ignore the hesitant knock on the door.

Tap, tap.

"Who is it?" Charlotte called out, not concealing her irritation.

The door opened slowly and one of the younger students warily poked her head inside. "Miss Brontë, you are wanted by Miss Wooler." The student's eyes widened as she took in Charlotte's disheveled appearance.

Miss Wooler was the headmistress at Roe Head. Charlotte quickly shoved her papers inside her folder. She stood up, smoothed her hair, and adjusted her skirts. "What does she want?"

The girl shook her head. "I don't know, Miss Brontë." She hesitated, then said in a hushed tone, "I think something might have happened to your sister."

In an instant, Charlotte forgot Angria and pushed past the student to run down the hall to Miss Wooler's office. She didn't breathe; she only ran. Who knew what might have happened to Emily? Lovely, reckless Emily, who thought she was invulnerable. "Let her be alive," Charlotte chanted under her breath.

When she arrived at Miss Wooler's door she knocked and entered in the same moment. "Miss Wooler, what's wrong? Is Emily all right?"

Sitting behind her wide desk, Miss Wooler narrowed her eyes at Charlotte's precipitous entrance. Charlotte glanced about frantically, exhaling in relief when her eyes lit upon Emily standing in a pool of light from the south-facing window. No matter what Emily had done, Charlotte reminded herself, her sister was alive.

Emily looked much the worse for wear. There were twigs and broken leaves trapped in her curls. A glance at Emily's hands revealed scratches and cuts.

Emily met her sister's gaze without a word. Charlotte's panic and concern warmed Emily in a way she found unexpected. But as Charlotte took in the situation, Miss Wooler's forbidding expression, and Emily's defiant stance, Emily saw the anxiety drain from her sister's face to be replaced by a mixture of impatience and exasperation. A look she had seen only too often.

"Miss Brontë, please come in," Miss Wooler said, a touch of sarcasm in her voice. "And Emily, step forward where I can see you."

Even seated, Miss Wooler was an imposing woman. Her massive desk suited her personality and her position. She wore her usual white wool gown, but unusually she was scowling. Charlotte thought the headmistress resembled a medieval abbess about to mete out judgment on an erring novice. And Emily? An impenitent through and through.

"Emily decided to leave Roe Head . . ." Miss Wooler began. "By way of a large oak tree."

Charlotte's mouth formed in an *O* but she couldn't manage to speak.

"The French mistress discovered her just as Emily was climbing out of the window. She tried to stop her, but Emily fell."

"From the second floor?" Charlotte asked, aghast. "You foolish girl!"

"It was her interference that made me fall," Emily interjected.

Charlotte edged closer to the desk. "Miss Wooler, I'm so sorry. She won't do it again."

"Thank you kindly for your concern, dear Charlotte," Emily said. She deliberately moved away from her sister. Why couldn't Charlotte take Emily's side, just once?

Miss Wooler contemplated both girls. Charlotte was tiny, not more than five feet, while Emily towered over her at almost half a foot taller. Charlotte stared into Miss Wooler's face, but was so shortsighted the headmistress didn't believe Charlotte could really see her clearly. Emily, on the other hand, looked down and away—a characteristic that in Miss Wooler's experience meant she was untrustworthy.

Miss Wooler's voice had iron in it. "Emily, you terrified Madame Librac. She thought you had fallen to your death."

"I'm perfectly capable of climbing down a tree," Emily retorted. Then she turned to Charlotte. "Tell her, Charlotte."

Charlotte ignored her.

"But why?" Miss Wooler asked, genuinely puzzled. "What could possibly warrant your running away?"

To Emily, Miss Wooler's direct question merited an honest answer. "I want to go home," Emily said, her eyes on her scuffed shoes.

"Oh, Emily!" Charlotte's voice was barely louder than an accusatory whisper. "You promised."

"I said I would *try*," Emily said. "But I don't like it here."

"Ah. You are homesick." Miss Wooler was on surer ground now. "That is a natural part of going to school. You will be stronger for having conquered it."

Charlotte willed Emily to keep quiet, knowing all the while that keeping Emily from speaking her mind was like asking the wind not to blow across Haworth Moor.

"What if I'm not interested in conquering my home-sickness, Miss Wooler?" Emily asked coolly.

"But Father wants you here," Charlotte interjected.

Keeping her eyes on Miss Wooler, who Emily knew ulti-mately would make the decision, Emily said, "Father wouldn't want me to stay here if he knew how unhappy I was." She stepped closer to Miss Wooler's desk and looked her straight in the eye. "I can't write here. I have no space to think. I don't fit here."

"Has anyone been unkind to you?" Miss Wooler asked. This was another problem she knew how to manage.

Emily looked blank. With a flash of irritated under-standing, Charlotte realized Emily wouldn't even notice any unkindness.

After a moment, Emily said, "Miss Wooler, wouldn't you rather have a student who chooses to be here?"

"Students do not dictate their desires to me," Miss Wooler answered. "In most cases, if a student did what you have done, I would send her home. But if I did that in this situation, I would be rewarding your bad behavior."

Charlotte shot Emily a triumphant glance. Miss Wooler was expressing Charlotte's sentiments exactly.

"I am not accustomed to failure." Miss Wooler went on. "You will stay and prosper. I will see to it personally."

"But . . ." Emily said.

Miss Wooler raised her hand to ward off any more argument. To Charlotte's surprise, Emily held her tongue. Miss Wooler said, "Emily, report to the infirmary and have those scratches seen to."

With a frustrated sigh, Emily stalked out of the room. Charlotte began to follow Emily, eager to scold her. Miss Wooler's voice stopped her in her tracks.

"Miss Brontë, a word, please."

Charlotte turned slowly, marshaling her arguments on behalf of Emily. "Miss Wooler, I assure you Emily will adjust. I, too, had difficulties when I arrived—but I became very happy here. She will, too."

"I did not call you back to speak about your sister." Miss Wooler's voice changed; suddenly she was no longer talking to a student but to an employee. "I wanted to talk about you."

Charlotte felt as though her stays in her bodice had been tightened, strangling her breath. "Me?" Her voice emerged as a squawk.

"You," Miss Wooler confirmed. "I hear . . . from several sources . . . you are not performing your duties to an adequate standard."

"Is this because I scolded Miss Lister? Her essay was not well written. I would have been remiss not to tell her so." Charlotte promised herself Miss Lister would soon see how strict Charlotte's standards could be.

"Miss Lister?" Miss Wooler picked up her pen and jotted down a few words on a piece of paper. "I've not spoken to her . . . yet. But some of the other teachers have expressed concern. They're worried the transition from student to teacher has proven too great a challenge. You seem distracted and unhappy."

Charlotte's hands twisted together, her fingers interlocking. "Miss Wooler, your informants are wrong. I am fine." Her chest felt tight and it was hard to breathe. "I love teaching, and I'm very grateful for the opportunity you have given me here." Miss Wooler watched her carefully. With a touch of desperation, Charlotte added, "I've been worried about Emily. She has been a source of great concern."

Miss Wooler clasped her hands and rested her chin on her fingers. "I want you to succeed, my dear. And not just for your sake, but for Emily's. I've never seen a girl in more need of discipline and rigorous study as she." As if she were thinking aloud, Miss Wooler said, "I know you and Emily have had an irregular upbringing. When I invited you to teach here, I did so despite my reservations about your father's political activities."

"Father?" Charlotte was astonished. "He's the reverend of Haworth and a learned and distinguished man of Cambridge."

"But also a Radical. I read his essays in the newspaper, railing against the Poor Laws and challenging the mill owners' right to conduct business as they see fit. Some of my students come from families who own mills. And their parents are concerned about your father's opinions."

"My father tells the truth even when it's not to his benefit," Charlotte said simply. "He's very brave."

"I see the apple did not fall far from the tree," Miss Wooler said. Charlotte's face warmed at the implied compliment. "Your sister Emily doesn't lack the courage of her convictions either. I've never seen a girl with so little concern for consequences."

Emily. Always Emily. In a flat voice, Charlotte said, "Yes. Father and Emily are very similar."

"But I digress," Miss Wooler said. "We were discussing your performance." She put her hands down flat on the desk and pushed herself to a standing position. Charlotte trembled as Miss Wooler came round to her side of the desk.

Charlotte waited, hardly daring to breathe. She could not, must not lose this position.

"As I said," Miss Wooler said, "I want you to succeed. It would be inconvenient to replace you. But if you cannot manage your teaching duties, I'll have to do without your services. And since your sister's tuition is part of your salary, Emily will have to go, too."

"Thank you, ma'am," Charlotte muttered and made her exit. In the hall, she leant against the door and tried to quell the shaking in her body.

Her nature proved here
too strong for her fortitude.

CHAPTER THREE

𝒞harlotte avoided Emily for a fortnight, trying instead to be the best teacher Miss Wooler had ever employed. To the extent she had considered Emily, she'd been relieved Emily had not caused any more trouble. But this evening, Charlotte had been summoned to the infirmary. Emily had fallen into a feverish sleep and could not be roused.

Emily writhed and moaned on the narrow sickbed. Charlotte placed her hand on Emily's forehead. The skin was hot, yet her face had a deathlike pallor that terrified Charlotte. She dipped a cloth in a basin of water, wrung it out, and lay it on Emily's brow.

The door swung open and Miss Wooler peeked inside. "How is she?" she asked.

Charlotte rushed to grasp Miss Wooler's hands. "She's burning up," she whispered.

Miss Wooler glided to Emily's bed and stared down at her. Her face was kind, but there was a hardness there, too. "We mustn't be precipitous. I'm sure it's just a mild fever." The only light in the room came from two candles on a table near Emily's bed; Miss Wooler's eyes reflected the twin flickering flames.

"I'm afraid she is truly ill. Emily never does anything by halves. We must call for a physician," Charlotte insisted. "Or send her home to be cared for by our family doctor."

The headmistress hesitated. "Are you certain she is really sick? Could this be a stratagem to go home?"

Charlotte froze. She hadn't considered that. Not even Emily would sink so low . . . would she?

She reached out and took Emily's hand. Her sister's skin, dry as parchment, perversely gave her courage to stand up to her employer. "Miss Wooler, what an outrageous accusation!" Charlotte answered, struggling to put assurance into her voice. "Even if Emily would fake her illness, do you believe I would connive at such a plan?"

Miss Wooler, her lips pursed, watched Charlotte's face. "No, I suppose you wouldn't."

"Thank you," Charlotte said.

"But even if she is not deliberately pretending, I've known unhappy students—not many, but a few—who were so unhappy they made themselves sick. They were looking for attention."

"Trust me, Emily is the last person to show off." Charlotte shook her head. "She cares nothing for the opinions of others, not even her family."

"How singular," Miss Wooler said with raised eyebrows. "But can we rule out a malady of the mind?" Her voice dropped to a whisper and her eyes darted to the door as if she feared eavesdroppers.

"Emily's illness may have started in her mind," Charlotte said firmly, "but she is physically ill now."

The wavering light cast a series of fantastic shadows on the whitewashed walls as Miss Wooler paced around the room. "If this is simply homesickness, sending her back would be doing her a great disservice; she might never leave home again."

Charlotte took a deep breath. It was time to use her strongest and most painful argument. "Please, Miss Wooler. I've lost two sisters already. I cannot lose another."

Miss Wooler stopped pacing. "How did they die?"

"Ten years ago they contracted consumption . . . while away at school."

Miss Wooler paled, no doubt considering the effect an outbreak of consumption would have on the reputation of her precious school. What parent would send their daughter to a school where she was likely to waste away of graveyard fever? "She doesn't have any of the symptoms . . . does she?"

"The disease attacks in so many different ways," Charlotte said. "I've seen it often in Haworth. I think we should call the doctor, just to be sure."

The headmistress made up her mind. "For the time being, you are excused from your teaching duties. Stay with Emily tonight. I'll send for the physician tomorrow morning."

"Thank you, Miss Wooler."

With a swish of her long skirts, Miss Wooler moved away, leaving Charlotte desolate at her sister's bed. Charlotte wished Emily would wake up so she could tell her that help was coming, but Emily's eyes remained stubbornly shut.

Charlotte drifted about the room, finally picking up Emily's small satchel. Many of the girls carried something like it to hold their books. Charlotte opened it and took out a novel by Sir Walter Scott, one of Emily's favorite authors. Emily couldn't resist the mesmerizing Scottish heroines who often as not rescued dashing soldiers.

As she fanned through the pages, a piece of paper fell to the floor. Curious, Charlotte picked it up, recognizing the handwriting. Anne, their youngest sister, had written it. Only fourteen, Anne had been very put out when Charlotte had campaigned for Emily to come to school. Her temper high, Anne had sworn never to forgive Charlotte for keeping her away from the excitement of school. Charlotte smiled at the memory. But Anne usually forgot her tempers in a few days. In fact, Charlotte was surprised Anne had not written to her yet.

Glancing at the bed to assure herself Emily still slept, she opened the letter and began to read.

Dearest Emily,

I shall confine my letter to a single page because I don't want you to have to pay the postman too much. I hope you're well. Even though she left me alone to die of boredom, I hope Charlotte is well, too.

Things are very dull in Haworth without you. Father is busier than ever now that so many men are out of work. When he isn't ministering to his flock, he is campaigning against injustice. Don't tell Charlotte, but he has begun to carry a pistol on his visits through the parish. It's an old-fashioned gun (Branwell told me, I don't pretend to know about such things), and once it is loaded, it can only be unloaded by firing the pistol. So every morning, we are awakened by the thunder of a gunshot. And you know how early Father wakes. Our few neighbors have all complained and Aunt Branwell is livid! But you know Father; once persuaded of his course, nothing can divert him.

Branwell has returned from London. His arrival was unexpected and mysterious. He won't tell anyone what happened at the Art Academy. Aunt B. thinks he discovered he wasn't good enough to be an artist. I think perhaps he fell in love with a lady of ill repute and spent all his money trying to win her heart only to be outbid by a rich lord. That would explain why he refuses to talk about it, don't you agree? Instead he mopes and grumbles about the house. He would be very depressing indeed if he didn't keep to his room so much.

Since you and Charlotte are gone until Christmas, I've decided to take up the invitation of Aunt B.'s bosom friend, Mrs. Leicester, in Scarborough. She is recuperating from a broken ankle and needs a young, lively presence to cheer her up (and no doubt fetch and carry and otherwise satisfy her every whim). Even if she is a perfect termagant, I shall still have some free time and I have always longed to see the sea. In all, I think it is an admirable way to spend the autumn. Of course Aunt B. is invited as well, but it would take a bog burst to shift her from the parsonage! So I will write again with my new address. Give my best to Charlotte, but tell her it is given only under duress!

Love, Anne

Postscript: Perhaps I underestimated how exciting it can be in Haworth. This afternoon a rock was thrown through our window! Father was angry but relieved no one was hurt. He is furious Grasper did not chase the miscreant. He said, "If this brute of Emily's can't even chase a vandal, what good is he?" But don't worry about Grasper; later I saw Father slip him a whole slice of Tabby's famous chocolate cake.

Charlotte smiled, picturing the scene. She refolded the letter and placed it back in the book. It was good to hear news from home, but why had no one written to her? She understood Anne was still out of sorts, but Father? Branwell? Aunt B.?

Suddenly Emily was sitting upright on the bed. "I can't breathe," she gasped. Charlotte rushed back to her sister in time to see her tossing the thick blanket to the floor.

Charlotte grabbed Emily's shoulders to press her back down to the mattress. The sharpness of the bones made her cringe. Charlotte pulled at her sister's chemise to reveal her bare shoulders and saw Emily's emaciated body. Emily had always been thin, but never like this. A wave of guilt swept Charlotte nearly off her feet. She had neglected her sister shamefully.

"The window!" Emily said.

Emily lived for fresh air, Charlotte knew, so she threw up the sash of the wide window. The temperature had dropped. Shivering, she glanced out at the line of enormous oak trees, whose wide leaves danced and bowed to the crescent moon.

Emily stared unseeingly toward the wide windows. "Maria! Elizabeth! You've finally come!"

Charlotte's veins ran ice. "Hush, dear. There's no one there."

"Have you come for me?" Emily cried to the air, extending her arms.

"Shhh, my dearest Emily," Charlotte begged. "Stay here with me. I know what's best for you."

"Don't you see them? They have been watching over me all this time."

"Be calm, Emily," Charlotte murmured as she took a wet cloth, wrung out the extra moisture, and laid it on Emily's fevered brow. "You're imagining our sisters are there. They aren't real."

"Sweet Maria and kind Elizabeth. They can't come in. You must open the window."

Charlotte's fear tasted like bile in her mouth. Struggling to keep her voice calm, she tried to reason her sister out of her delusion. "The windows *are* open," she said. "If they chose, they could enter. Perhaps they aren't yet ready to visit."

Emily collapsed back to the bed, tears running down her cheeks. "Are they waiting for me to die?"

"Hush, do not speak of death. Rest." She rubbed Emily's cold hand, noticing the raised goose bumps on her sister's flesh. "Do you feel the freshness of the wind?"

"It is not our north wind sweeping across the moors," Emily moaned. "This wind is too tame."

A stray gust extinguished the candles. Charlotte gasped, but Emily didn't notice.

Charlotte crawled into bed and pulled the blanket over both of them. "The moors are not so far," she said. "Twenty miles away at most. I'll bring you there when term ends in December."

"I'll be dead before then," Emily said, rolling over to turn her face to the wall.

"No!" Charlotte cried, but deep in her bones, she feared if Emily didn't go home, she would die.

"I will save you," Charlotte vowed. "You will walk on the moors again."

[she] said she was ill; at which I hardly wondered.
I informed Mr. Heathcliff and he replied,—
"Well, let her till after the funeral; and go up now
and then to get her what is needful;
and, as soon as she seems better, tell me."

CHAPTER FOUR

*E*mily paced about the square parlor of the parsonage like a wild animal exploring the limits of her cage. "I'm feeling much better, Aunt B.," she said for the fourth time. "It can't hurt me to go outside. Just for a little time."

Aunt B. finished draping her black silk shawl across her round shoulders. She adjusted her old-fashioned cap to display her false hairpiece of auburn curls across her forehead. She was dressed for a funeral next door at the Old Church, although privately Emily didn't think her outfit differed all that much from the dark clothes her aunt usually wore in the house.

"No, Emily, dear. The doctor said you are to rest for several more days."

"I've been resting since I got home. It's been ten days!" Emily protested. She ran her fingers through her hair; thank goodness the detested curls were growing out.

"And the doctor said a fortnight." Aunt B. pulled on her gloves. "There's the church bell. Your father is starting the service punctually."

"When isn't he punctual?" Emily asked. She glanced out the window. "There are still people coming. Whose funeral warrants such a good turnout?"

"Hush, Emily, don't be common. It's one of your father's deacons. I can't recall which. But since you are ill and Charlotte and Anne are away, your father especially asked me to attend to represent the family."

"What about Branwell?" Emily asked, a hint of spite in the question. Branwell had not been notable lately for honoring his familial obligations.

"He promised to be there as well." Aunt B. went to the front door. "Now, my dear, make sure you rest. Because the deceased was a deacon, your father will invite the other deacons here for tea. Would you like to dress properly and act as your father's hostess?"

Emily, in her dressing gown, took a step backward. "Heavens, no! Aunt B., how could you think it of me?"

With satisfaction, Aunt B. said, "Then go to bed." Suddenly she bellowed, "Tabby! Tabby!"

The family housekeeper came into the room. A stout Yorkshirewoman with pale skin and a broad face, Tabby had worked for the Brontë family for more than a decade. "Yes, ma'am?" she asked with a scowl.

"Make sure Emily doesn't leave the house. Is the tea ready? Don't be too generous with the cream. The deacons are the ones who vote on the reverend's salary, and we don't want them to think we are profligate. Add some ale, too. After this funeral, some will ask for spirits."

"I'll need the keys," Tabby said sourly.

Emily hid a smile behind her hand. This particular battle had raged since the day Tabby arrived. Aunt B. didn't trust a mere servant with the cellar keys, and Tabby deeply resented Aunt B.'s lack of confidence. Aunt B. hesitated, then took a key ring from her skirt pocket.

"See that you give the keys to Emily when you are finished," she warned.

"Of course, ma'am," Tabby said. Then in a whisper just out of Aunt B.'s limited range of hearing, she added, "If I'm not too drunk to remember."

With a little wave, Aunt B. opened the door and was gone.

"That woman!" Tabby exclaimed. "How dare she act like I'm a closet drunkard? It's just as well she hardly comes out of her room anymore. Otherwise, it would be her or me!"

"We'd choose you and your apple tarts anytime, dear Tabby," Emily said. She went to the window to watch Aunt B. join the late arrivals and enter the church.

Since Aunt B. lived almost entirely in her room, Emily spent much more time with Tabby in her warm kitchen smelling of delicious food and parish gossip. Emily had become a fair cook herself, often propping up a novel to read while she stirred a stew or kneaded the bread.

"Tabby, who is Father burying?" Emily asked, certain the housekeeper would know the answer.

"Old Mr. Heaton, the master of Ponden Hall," Tabby answered promptly.

Ponden Hall was a manor not two miles from the parsonage, due west across the moors. "I remember Ponden Hall," Emily exclaimed. "Mr. Heaton used to let us visit the library once a week. It was beautiful, with leather-bound books from floor to ceiling and a wonderful armchair just in front of the fire." She paused. "Why did we stop going? I can't remember."

"Your father and Mr. Heaton had a bit of a falling-out," Tabby said, wiping the dining table with her rag. "After that, the reverend discouraged you from going."

"There was a boy there . . . about Charlotte's age." The memory of a pale face with piercing blue eyes came into her mind. "He wasn't strong. I always found him in the library. Sometimes even if he wasn't there, he suddenly appeared like a character in a pantomime! It was uncanny."

Tabby snorted, her habitual response to Emily's flights of fancy. "No doubt you had your nose buried so deep in a book you didn't hear him coming."

"No doubt." Emily tilted her head as though to peer into the past. "I wonder what happened to him. He vanished not long before we stopped going to Ponden Hall." Out the window, she saw the last of the parishioners entering the church.

"I wager the service will be short," Tabby muttered. "No one will say a kind word about old Mr. Heaton, except your father."

Emily looked alert. "Truly? Then perhaps the tea might be more interesting than I thought. Perhaps I should get dressed?"

Tabby shook her head. "The gossip you're likely to hear isn't suitable."

"Tell me!" Emily plopped herself down on the scratchy horsehair sofa. "First, how did he die?"

Tabby went to the hall and glanced up and down, even though the house was empty. Then she scurried back and sat down knee to knee with Emily. "That's the question. They say he fell off his horse."

"If that's what they say aloud," Emily said, "then what are they whispering?"

"Old Mr. Heaton was a fiend on horseback. He rode everywhere and had nary an accident his whole life. He only has the one son, Master Robert, and they've never gotten along. Like chalk and cheese, those two. Mr. Heaton liked things the way they were while his son wanted to make the mills and the farms more modern. Words were exchanged, I hear. Then the two men went out riding and only one came back!"

"*Definitely* suspicious," Emily said delightedly. "But it's just talk, I'm sure."

Tabby shook her head and her generous bosom quivered. "'Tis a fact young Master Heaton had gambling debts before his father died. And old Mr. Heaton refused to help him. Now, Master Robert has all the money, the farms, and the mills."

"What did the constable say about the accident?" Emily asked.

"People like the Heatons have the law in their pockets," Tabby said with narrowed eyes. "Without proof, the constable wouldn't even ask any questions." She pushed herself up out of the chair. "Now, Miss Emily, let's get you to bed before anybody sees you in your dressing gown. What would people think?"

"That you and Aunt B. and Dr. Bennett both worry over-much and refuse to let me go outside!" But because she loved Tabby, she let the housekeeper lead her upstairs.

"You were so thin when you came back from that awful school. Like a wraith," Tabby said, her eyes tearing up. "So you'll stay in bed until you're healthy again. We can't lose you like . . ." Her voice trailed off as they reached Emily's bedroom.

Emily ducked under Tabby's arm and went into her tiny room. "Like Maria and Elizabeth?" As she always did when she thought of her lost sisters, she glanced at the cemetery outside the window. All these years later, she still hoped if she watched at just the right time, she would see her sisters' spirits hovering.

"Poor girls." Tabby nodded heavily. "All this education is bad for your health. I don't know what Miss Charlotte was thinking, letting you get so ill. That one always thinks she knows what's best with her high-and-mighty bossing."

Emily hesitated, but then the true story escaped her lips. "Tabby, that's not fair. Charlotte tried to keep me out of trouble. And she's the one who convinced the headmistress to send me home." Then with a grimace she added, "But her high-handedness is infuriating, isn't it?"

"She's as bad as your Aunt B." Tabby clapped her hand over her mouth. Between her fingers, she said, "Forget I said that!" As she turned to leave, she added, "Mind you close that window."

The bells rang outside, and Emily climbed up on the window seat to see the church entrance. She stuck her head outside the windowsill. "That was quick," she said. She spied a small man with a shock of curly red hair. "Look, Branwell did go to the funeral. He's talking with John Brown and one of the mourners." Brown was her father's sexton, the man who maintained the church and dug all the graves.

"Your father will be pleased," Tabby said. "Your brother's been moping about the house like a chicken who knows the ax is coming." Casually she looked over Emily's shoulder. "That's the heir, young Robert Heaton."

"Do they know each other?"

Tabby shrugged. "Your brother keeps his own counsel. If the service is over, I'd best be getting tea ready." She hurried out.

Emily lay in her bed with the door ajar. She listened to the arrivals and the sound of self-important men drinking their tea and ale. Her father's voice, always distinctive and authoritative, occasionally rose above the rest.

After a time, the front door opened and she heard some of the guests take their leave. Suddenly she was surprised to hear voices on the second floor, not far from her room.

"Our brother the Worshipful Master has asked me to be your sponsor," a deep voice said.

"I'd be honored, sir." It was the quick, anxious voice of her brother, Branwell.

"Perhaps we can talk privately," the first voice said. "There are certain tasks you must perform before your initiation."

"My room is down this passage," Branwell said.

"What about your father's study? It would be more suitable."

There was a long pause. Emily listened intently for the next words. Finally Branwell said, "I'm not permitted in my father's study alone. None of us are."

With a nonchalance that seemed forced to Emily's ear, the other man said, "No matter. To your room, then."

Emily scrambled out of bed and rushed to her door. As cautious as a cat, she lifted the latch and peered down the hall. But she was too late. Branwell had already let his mysterious guest precede him into the room. But some small sound must have alerted her brother, for Branwell's head jerked sharply in her direction. He murmured something to his guest, then came marching down the hallway.

"Go to bed, Emily. My business is none of your concern." He shoved her inside the room and pulled the door closed.

Leaning against her bedroom door, Emily murmured, "Branwell has a secret."

But it was one of their chief amusements to
run away to the moors in the morning and
remain there all day, and the after punishment
grew a mere thing to laugh at.

CHAPTER FIVE

*T*he household had long ago gone to bed but Emily paced around her bedroom, her long stride making the tiny room even smaller. The doctor had confined her to the house for a fortnight and her sentence was up tomorrow, but she felt as though she were overflowing with energy. She feared she might explode if she didn't go outside. Despite her assurances that she was completely recovered, Father and Aunt B. still forbade Emily to walk on the moors. They did not understand Emily required physical exercise, not only for her body but also for her mind.

The full moon shone directly into Emily's room through the open window and the chilly air burned her lungs. Outside the window, the branches of the cherry tree made a pleasing pattern against the glowing orb.

When Emily was a child, she had climbed that tree more than once. Years ago, Emily and Branwell had often played Pirate King, with Emily forever in the role of the hostage doomed to walk the plank by venturing out on the tree limb. The game had ended when Emily surprised Branwell by nimbly climbing down the tree to freedom. Her tongue darted across her lips. She had eluded captivity before; why not now?

A fast-moving cloud traversing the moon seemed like a signal. Clad only in her nightdress, Emily hurriedly wrapped her shabby shawl around her shoulders. She slipped on her walking shoes without taking the time to put on her stockings and then clambered over the windowsill.

Half climbing, half falling, she made it to the ground and ran to the garden gate. Glancing back at the parsonage, she reassured herself the house was still undisturbed. Slowly she opened the gate, wincing at the loud creak.

Emily hurried along the gravel path between the parsonage garden's stone wall and the row of tall trees on the other side. The cool night air caressed her skin and the north wind felt like a familiar friend's embrace. Even in the darkness, her feet had not forgotten the way up the steep hill marking the end of the churchyard and the beginning of the moors. At the top, she reluctantly stopped, her hand pressed against a stitch in her side. It had been too long.

Her breath recaptured, Emily gasped in delight when the moon reappeared and illuminated the vast moor unfolding itself like a carpet being rolled out for her pleasure. The wind caught the fullness of her nightdress and it billowed out around her knees like the plumage of some fantastic bird. The scent of heather and bracken, mixed with a coming storm, was better for her health than all the elixirs and medicaments they had forced down her throat.

Holding her arms out wide, she hurtled down the path, away from Haworth. She had no purpose and no destination, like a tuft of cotton grass being tossed on the air currents. She laughed out loud from the sheer joy of being outside and unaccounted for. Finally she came to a favorite rock. It was shaped like an armchair, and Emily often stopped there with a book. She climbed onto it, ignoring the damp chill of the stone through her cotton nightdress.

Emily stared at the brilliant stars, clearly visible in the clean, crisp night air. Her attention was captured closer to earth when she saw a light flicker across the moor.

"Who would be out at this hour?" Eyes trained on the light, she headed across the moor once again. If her sister Charlotte were here, she would be tugging on her sleeve to lead Emily back to the safety of the beaten path. Tabby would warn Emily of the hazards of following a will-o'-the-wisp, whispering tales of travelers being led fatally astray by malicious spirits. And Father? He would worry about human villains. Emily thought it was just as well none of them was here, because she saw only the possibility of adventure.

Without the full moon, even Emily would not have been able to navigate the boulders and bracken littering the moor like a giant's abandoned toys. As she closed in on the light, Emily saw it was a small campfire in a hollow tucked underneath the shelter of a small bluff, sparks flying into a pool of darkness beyond.

Careful to keep her steps soundless, Emily crept closer. Suddenly an enormous creature leapt in front of Emily. She cried out and stumbled back, falling heavily to the ground. The beast growled deep in its throat, louder than her beating heart.

It was a dog, a mastiff, easily outweighing Emily. His huge fangs glistened and his eyes glowed red from the fire's reflection. Trembling from head to toe, she forced herself to be perfectly still.

"Gently, boy," Emily whispered.

Slowly she got to her knees, keeping a close eye on the animal. Careful not to make eye contact, knowing this would seem like a challenge, Emily reached out a hand, palm first. He bared his teeth and growled again.

"Shh, boy, I'm no danger to you," Emily said in her most soothing voice. She kept her hand extended. The dog sniffed, and after a moment to consider, he licked her palm. Emily stroked his nose. He nuzzled against her, almost knocking her over with his bulk. Fondling the sagging skin around his neck and jowls, she whispered, "Good boy, I know we'll be friends."

The dog barked. Emily shushed him, but then, tail wagging, the dog barked louder. The noise rolled along the moors, echoing in the darkness.

"Who's there?" A man's voice called out. On the far side of the fire, Emily saw a silhouette in a long cloak.

"Show yourself!" he shouted.

Emily might have spoken up, but then she heard the unmistakable click of a cocking pistol. Without another moment's hesitation, she scrambled to her feet and fled. The dog didn't follow but set up a fusillade of barking. With no time to pick out the best path, Emily tripped and stumbled in the underbrush.

"Stop," yelled the man.

Emily ran. The prickly gorse caught her nightdress and held her back. Emily thrashed at the sharp bushes until she could tear herself free. She saw the hill leading back to the parsonage and she pushed herself to run faster.

Her eyes fixed on the slope, she didn't see the hollow in the ground at her feet. She fell headlong, knocking the breath from her body. She listened, struggling to hear over her labored breathing.

There. Emily heard the sound of footsteps, distant enough, but still coming toward her. A thud and a muffled curse told Emily her pursuer was suffering from the whims of the moor, just as she was.

She got to her feet and mustered all her strength for the final hill. At the crest, she looked down to see the parsonage ahead, beckoning her to safety. Behind her, the stranger was just starting to race up the hill. He wasn't far behind.

Emily flung herself down the hill until she reached the parsonage gate. Her fingers fumbled as she undid the gate's latch, but at last it was open and she practically fell into the garden. She only had to shout and Father would rescue her. She peered through the gate, but saw no sign of her pursuer. Emily sucked air into her lungs and let her thudding heart realize she was safe.

A man's hand grabbed her shoulder. Emily screamed.

It's a pity he cannot kill himself with drink.

CHAPTER SIX

$\mathcal{G}$et away from me!" Emily jerked away from the grip on her shoulder. "I'll call my father. He has a pistol!"

"Shhh, Emily . . . for God's sake, be quiet!" The voice at her elbow was slurred but familiar. "I know Father has a pistol."

Emily's voice shook until she got it under control. "Branwell? Why were you chasing me?"

"What?" Her brother slumped against the stone wall. The moonlight lit up his red hair like a beacon. "Em, what are you doing here? Were you waiting up for me?" Pushing himself away from the wall, he threw his arms around her. "I knew you still cared."

Now the danger was past, her legs could hardly support her. She looked down on Branwell's head, sniffed, and wrinkled her nose. "Oh, Branwell, you're drunk again."

Branwell blinked behind his spectacles. "I'm not drunk." He scowled suspiciously. "Were you following me?"

"I just needed some air." Before Emily could finish her explanation, Branwell's mouth started working and his eyes bulged. Without any further warning, he vomited all over her shoes.

"Branwell! That's dreadful!" Emily shoved him away from her. He stumbled over to the wall, fell to his knees, and lost the rest of his stomach contents. She shook off her shoes and brushed the disgusting chunks from her nightdress. Her mouth twisted to avoid vomiting, too.

She stood over him, pinching her nostrils at the stench. "What am I going to do with you?" she scolded. "It's the middle of the night. I've half a mind to wake Father and let him deal with you."

"Em, don't let him see me like this," Branwell pleaded.

"Where have you been?"

He rubbed his eyes with the palms of his hands. "I was with some friends at the snug."

The snug was the private room at the Black Bull Tavern, just down the hill. Branwell was too often to be found there. In recent years, disappointment and drink had dulled the brilliance of the bold twelve-year-old pirate who had been

Emily's nemesis and playmate. Self-pity had worn away all his promise.

"And . . ." Emily's voice trailed off expectantly.

"Then we went to a boxing match." He rubbed the back of his neck. Emily knew his telltale signs of guilt.

"Was there gambling at the match?" she asked, dreading the answer.

Shamefaced, he nodded. "I lost the money Father gave me."

Emily caught her breath. "But he gave you two whole pounds!"

"I can count, little sister." Branwell wouldn't meet her eyes.

Emily thought of how many books she could buy with so much money and shook her head.

"I don't need your disapproval, too," Branwell said. "I get more than enough from Father and Charlotte. But you're different—you accept me as I am." Even in a whisper, she could hear the charm in his coaxing. "Be a love and let me in the house," he said. "All the doors are locked."

"What's to stop me from finding my own way in and leaving you out in the cold?" Emily retorted.

"Nothing," Branwell said. "Just as there's nothing to prevent me from telling Father I found you outside at this hour."

Emily had to clap her hands over her mouth to keep from laughing out loud. "Branwell, you're the one who's drunk and sick and will have to explain your gambling losses. My crimes are minor in comparison."

Branwell took off his spectacles and cleaned them with the bottom of his shirt that had escaped his trousers. "We both know I won't be punished. But Father would keep you from the moors for months."

Emily scowled. Branwell was right. If Father knew Emily had disobeyed him, he would keep her inside indefinitely.

"Just a minute." She went back to her tree. Looking up at the window to her room, it seemed impossibly high although she knew she'd done it before. If only she were not so tired.

Pushing away her fatigue, she began to climb. In an instant, she was dragging herself over the windowsill into her bedroom. She hurried downstairs to draw back the long iron bolt and lift the latch.

Branwell was waiting outside the door. He staggered inside. "I'm hungry," he said. "And thirsty."

"There's a pitcher of fresh water in the larder, and Tabby made you a plate since you missed dinner."

"Aren't you going to serve me?" he asked querulously.

"Why would I?"

"Because I am the son of the house and you're just a girl."

"Save that for the unfortunate woman you marry. You're not my lord and master." Now she was within the closeness of the house, Emily felt exhaustion creeping into her limbs. "I'm going to bed."

"You've a cold heart to abandon me after the night I've had," he whined.

"I'm tired," Emily said. She glanced to the clock on the stair landing, illuminated by the moonlight streaming in the window. "It's past midnight."

"Give your brother an arm," Branwell pleaded. "Help me get to bed."

She crinkled her nose. "I think not. You reek of spirits, tobacco, and worse." Making sure the front door was firmly shut and locked, she turned to go upstairs.

"You needn't be so high and mighty," he accused, deliberately blocking her way.

Placing a palm flat against his chest, Emily pushed him easily against the wall. "Don't try to bully me. I trounced you when we were children and I still can."

"That you can, dear sister." It was one of Branwell's many grievances that of all Rev. Brontë's children, only Emily had inherited their father's height. And Tabby thought Emily might grow still taller, if only she would eat more.

Branwell slid down the wall until he was sitting, miserable, on the cold stone floor. In the darkness, Emily heard him sob. "What kind of man am I?"

"Whatever kind of man you choose to be," Emily said, not unkindly. "If you like, I'll try imagining who you should be."

"I'm not a character in one of your stories," Branwell said scornfully.

"No, my heroes behave much worse," Emily said with a crooked grin. "Good night." Without a backward glance, she ran up the stairs on silent feet.

"Em, at least give me a candle!" Branwell's despairing whisper dogged her heels up the stairs.

Emily didn't stop. If only she could stay awake a little longer, she longed to write. Her adventures tonight were good enough for her next story. She just had to make sure her father never read it.

I surveyed the weapon inquisitively.
A hideous notion struck me: how powerful
I should be possessing such an instrument!

CHAPTER SEVEN

The sound of glass breaking entered Emily's dream and tugged her back to consciousness. It seemed like only minutes since she had laid her head on her pillow. She heard her father shouting but she couldn't make out the words. Fully awake now, she held her breath so she could listen. The sky outside her window was completely black; the moon was gone but dawn had not yet arrived.

Suddenly a pistol shot startled Emily upright. The noise made even the sturdy parsonage shake.

"What was that noise?" Her aunt's frightened voice filled the house. "Patrick! Branwell!"

Emily scrambled out of bed, nearly falling to the floor in her haste. She rushed into the hallway. Her aunt was waving a candle wildly. Her pale face, looking oddly naked without its false fringe of hair, wore a terrified expression. "Thank goodness you are safe, Emily. Where is your father? Where's your brother?"

Placing her arm around her aunt's shoulders, Emily said, "I'm sure everyone is fine." But Emily's heart tightened with fear. "Father! Where are you?"

"Emily!" Her father called from downstairs. "Are you all right?"

"Stay here, Aunt B.," Emily said. Without waiting for her aunt's response, she charged down the stairs. The house was dark, but she could make out her father's tall figure in the doorway to his study.

"Father!" Emily cried. "Did you fire that shot?"

"Yes," he said, and his breathing was ragged as though he had been running. He moved into his office and found the lamp on his desk. Emily could see his hand tremble as he lit the wick. "I was asleep when I heard the sound of breaking glass in my office," he went on. "So I came downstairs to investigate."

"You shouldn't have come down alone," Emily said. "You might have been killed."

"I saw a figure reaching in to unlatch the window." Her father pointed to the shattered windowpane. "I warned him I was armed . . . then I fired!" Rev. Brontë sank into his chair and put his head in his hands. "I don't know if I hit him or not, but he didn't get into the house."

The horror on Emily's face was reflected on his. Her father's eyesight was impaired by milky white cataracts that grew thicker every year. What if he had killed a man? They could lose everything. She ran out into the hall and threw open the front door.

"Emily! Don't go outside!" her father called.

Emily paused to ensure the garden was deserted. Then she hurried to the flowerbed in front of her father's study. She squinted at the ground covered with green moss, afraid of what she might see.

Nothing. No one was there, dead or even wounded. Emily put her hand to the sill and let herself breathe. "Father," she called into the study through the broken window. "You missed! There's nothing here," she said, her voice full of relief. The moss did not take any footprints, so there was nothing to be learned from the ground.

"Thank God," he said.

She went back inside and took her father's lamp off the desk to better examine the windowsill. She touched her finger to some spatters on the wood. They were fresh and bloody. She started to tell her father, then thought better of it. It was most likely the burglar had cut his hand when he broke the glass, but perhaps her father had only slightly missed.

She held up the lamp to the wall near the window. A bullet hole in the window sash bore witness to the reverend's lack of marksmanship.

She turned to her father. "Did you see who it was?"

He shook his head. "It was too dark." Recovering his composure, Rev. Brontë said, "I always told your aunt it was a sensible precaution to have a pistol in the house." Emily ducked her head to hide her smile at his smug tone.

Emily's hand went to her lips. "Aunt B.! I left her upstairs."

"Branwell is taking care of her, no doubt," her father said.

Emily had plenty of doubt that Branwell could take care of himself, least of all anyone else. "I'll go see," she offered. She ran upstairs and found Aunt B. in Branwell's room, staring at Emily's unconscious brother sprawled half on and half off his bed, wearing only his trousers. His snoring was loud enough to drown out almost anything except a pistol shot.

"Is your father all right?" Aunt B. asked, her quavering voice full of anxiety.

Emily nodded.

"Thank goodness." Her voice lost the worry and became censorious as she pointed at Branwell. "He's been indulging again, hasn't he?"

Emily shrugged. "Ask him yourself when he wakes." She led Aunt B. by the elbow to the landing.

Rev. Brontë was waiting for them, his lantern throwing elongated shadows on the wall. "Where is your brother?" he asked quietly, as though he feared the answer.

Before Emily could frame an answer, her aunt interrupted. "Patrick, the boy is inebriated!"

"Emily?" he asked. She nodded reluctantly.

"God does not give us burdens we cannot bear," he murmured. Placing the lamp on the hall table, he put his hands on Aunt B.'s shoulders. "Now you must go back to bed. The excitement is over." He gently pushed her toward her room. Over his shoulder, he said, "Emily, you, too. We'll talk in the morning."

Emily obediently returned to her own room and climbed back into bed. She tried to put her thoughts in order. Who would try to break into the parsonage? And why? Try as she might, she could think of nothing worth stealing. She did have a clue she could use to identify the intruder: He had cut himself. She would be on the lookout for any bandaged hands or forearms.

Suddenly her eyes flew open. Could the attempted break-in have something to do with her misadventure on the moor? Was that mysterious man wrapping up a bleeding cut at this very moment? Should she tell her father? But how could she, when her father had forbidden her to go out?

As she drifted into sleep, she spared a thought for Branwell. If he wasn't careful he was going to break their father's heart.

When morning finally came, the reverend did not fire his usual pistol shot. Emily only awoke when she heard Tabby's voice in her aunt's room next door. Tabby's room was on the opposite side of the house and could only be reached from the garden. A sound sleeper, she must have slept through the hubbub. No doubt Aunt B. was telling Tabby everything.

Emily stretched her long arms over her head, frowning at the scratches from the brambles on the moor. Suddenly she realized evidence of her nighttime wandering was everywhere. She had to conceal it from Tabby. She shoved the dirt-stained nightdress and vomit-stained shoes behind her tiny wardrobe just in time. A knock on the door and Tabby entered.

"Good morning, Tabby," Emily said breathlessly.

"Good morning! Is that all you can say, Miss Emily? When according to your aunt we all might have been killed in our beds?" Tabby said, depositing a ewer filled with warm water on the small table.

"The burglar didn't even come into the house, Tabby. We were never in danger."

"I can't believe I didn't wake," Tabby sniffed. "Well, it's after six o'clock. Your father is already moving about in his room, so I'll have to wait until after prayers to hear more."

"I'll be there in a moment," Emily assured her. No sooner had Tabby closed the door than Emily was washing quickly with a rough facecloth dipped in the warm water, making sure to get the dirt from under her fingernails. In the same rapid manner, she dressed, shoved her feet into house slippers, and raced down the hall for morning prayers in her father's bedroom.

Her father was on his knees, his thick white hair slicked down on his skull like a cap of snow. Emily took her place between Tabby and Aunt B. Branwell was conspicuously absent, but Rev. Brontë didn't remark on his dereliction.

"Amen."

Emily's eyes, dutifully closed during her father's lengthy prayer, flew open on the final word. Rev. Brontë closed the Bible and stood up without effort despite his sixty-odd years. His habit of walking miles each day was serving his aging body well; he was fitter than many men half his age.

As if with one mind, Emily and Tabby each took one of Aunt B.'s arms and helped her to her feet.

"Well said, Patrick," Aunt B. said in her raspy whisper. "I will miss your sermons while I'm away."

Emily looked at her aunt sharply, but her surprise was nothing to Rev. Brontë's. "You're going away? What do you mean?" he asked.

"Aunt, you never go away," Emily said.

"After last night's fright, I've decided to join Anne in Scarborough. The sea air will do me good."

Emily thought gleefully of the freedom she would have without Aunt B.'s watchful eye upon her. Tabby looked alert, like a cat that has spied a plump mouse.

"For how long?" The reverend's voice was incredulous and perhaps the least bit hopeful. Aunt B. had arrived ten years ago when her sister, the children's mother, was ill. After her sister's death, Aunt B. had stayed on to help raise the children, and never left.

"A few weeks. Hopefully by then, all this fuss will have died down," Aunt B. said.

"When do you plan to go?" Emily asked.

"Tomorrow." Aunt B. raised a palm. "Now, before you say it is too soon, let me tell you I couldn't sleep last night and I'm already packed." She added, "I've only to write to my friend Mrs. Leicester in Scarborough, and put a few things in my valise." She returned to her bedroom, her wooden shoes making a familiar clopping sound on the flagstone floor.

Downstairs at the table, Emily and the reverend waited for Tabby to serve their breakfast. Glancing about to ensure no one could overhear, he quietly asked Emily, "How late was Branwell out last night?"

"He came home before I went to bed, Father." Her nose wrinkled at the memory. Before he could ask for particulars, she elaborated. "He was very merry, but tired." Emily congratulated herself for walking a delicate line between her loyalty to her brother and telling her father the truth, all without revealing she had been outside herself.

"No doubt he had been drinking with some of his new friends. I've always believed giving my children complete freedom was the right thing to do—but Branwell's behavior is worrisome." Rev. Brontë's worried eyes sought reassurance from his daughter.

"I'm certain he will be sorry to have missed the excitement last night. And morning prayers," Emily said noncommittally. Under her breath, she added, "Again."

Rev. Brontë sighed. Tabby bustled in with a tray.

"Tabby, please prepare a glass of sugar water with twelve drops of ammonia in it. Leave it by Branwell's bed."

Emily made a face. "That sounds vile, Father."

"My copy of *Modern Domestic Medicine* says it will help a headache from overindulging."

Tabby scowled. "That book is full of nonsense."

"Nevertheless I would like you to do as I ask," Rev. Brontë ordered.

Tabby sniffed, but said nothing. A moment later she had placed steaming mugs of tea and bowls of rich porridge in front of them. She gave Emily a jar of her special marmalade. Emily opened the jar and scooped several spoonfuls into her porridge.

"Greedy child," Tabby scowled.

Emily didn't take offence. Tabby pretended to scold Emily but was delighted when Emily gobbled down the jam. It was her personal ambition to fatten Emily up. Indeed, since her return from school, Emily had plumped up like a bullfrog's throat. "I can't help it. It's delicious." Emily said as she energetically stirred the sticky marmalade into the porridge.

"Just so long as you don't feed it to that dog of yours." The oft-repeated scold slipped out of Tabby's mouth before she could stop herself. Tabby dropped the ladle to the table and clapped her hands across her mouth. "Emily, I'm so sorry. I forgot."

Emily's eyes filled with tears, but she hastened to reassure Tabby. "I forget, too." Grasper, her beloved dog, had died from a surfeit of cake a few days before Emily's return. Rev. Brontë had not known dogs couldn't eat chocolate.

Her father hurried to change the subject. "Tabby, send for the glazier to fix the window today, please."

"Of course, reverend."

After Tabby left, Emily asked, "Will you send for the constable?"

He nodded. "But I doubt he'll be able to learn anything about last night. He's been no help whatsoever with the other odd happenings. Did Tabby tell you a rock was thrown through our front window?"

"Anne wrote to me about it," Emily said. "Do you think your burglar has something do with that?"

Rev. Brontë shrugged. "I've received some threats in the mail because of my support for the millworkers. Perhaps he was going to vandalize my office? Maybe he thought there might be something valuable in the study," he said doubtfully. "Little did he know there's naught but parish records and my correspondence."

"Who would bother stealing those musty papers?" Emily asked.

"They are important, but not worth anything," her father answered. "But Rev. Smythe in Bradford had a burglar too and his register of marriages was stolen. Strange things are afoot on the moor these days."

There was a silence while they ate their breakfast. When the reverend pushed away his empty plate, he asked, "What are you going to do this morning?"

Emily shrugged. "After my chores, I'll take a long ramble, I suppose."

Rev. Brontë frowned, and Emily hurried to remind him that the doctor's prescription of two weeks' rest was complete.

"It's not that, Emily; I'm concerned about you walking on the moors alone," he said. "After last night . . ."

"I'm perfectly safe, Father." Remembering her headlong flight the night before, she could feel the heat on her cheeks. "I thought I would go as far as Ponden Hall and back. That's only four miles."

"I'd rather you avoided the Heaton lands altogether. There's been uncharitable talk about Mr. Heaton's death."

Emily nodded. "Tabby told me. But why should that affect my walk?"

"I've heard about a strange man lurking near Ponden Hall. I was talking with young Robert Heaton at his father's funeral." He stopped to shake his head sadly. "He was barely civil to me, I'm afraid, even though I was burying his father. He's leading the mill owners against the workers. He practically threatened me if I didn't stop writing my editorials."

"And the stranger—" Emily prompted. She had already heard about her father's political problems in the parish.

"Heaton complained about a man often lurking about the farm. When Heaton rides out to confront him—he's gone."

The stranger must be the man who chased her the night before. Emily leaned in, her elbows on the table. "How fascinating. I wonder what he wants?"

"If it *is* a man," Tabby said darkly. She had been listening from the door. Rev. Brontë opened his mouth to remonstrate, then closed it again.

"Tabby, do you think it's a woman?" Emily asked. From her own memory, she didn't think it could have been, but her imagination ran away with the idea. "She might have been a noble lady who was seduced by old Mr. Heaton. She startled him while he was riding and that's how he died. She's so guilt-stricken she has to haunt his estate."

"My clever Emily, how do you think of these things?" Rev. Brontë smiled indulgently. "But Mr. Heaton said his trespasser was a man."

Tabby, as though she was just waiting for the opportunity, slid back a chair and settled herself at the table. "Neither man nor woman, I'll wager. Not even human! Grace, the house-keeper at Ponden, told me a huge dog roams the estate at night."

"So?" Emily asked, recalling the mastiff's rough tongue on her palm.

"Miss Emily, it's a ghost dog, with red glowing eyes and fangs dripping blood!"

The reverend struggled to keep a straight face. "Don't be absurd, Tabby!"

Tabby shook her head with eyes narrowed in warning of some disastrous presentiment. "Laugh if you like, but I'll wager you my next apple pie the stranger and the dog are one and the same. It's a *gytrash*! That's why Mr. Heaton cannot find the man. He transforms into the dog whenever Mr. Heaton comes near."

At the mention of the mythological monster, the reverend nearly choked on his toast. "Tabby—I forbid you to talk any more of monsters. There is enough superstition and blasphemy out there without inviting them into the parsonage."

Emily was silent as she reviewed the events of the night before. The man and the dog were definitely two separate creatures.

"Emily, whatever is out there is real. If you must walk alone, I think we should get another dog. One of my parishioners has some terrier puppies. I will ask if we can buy one."

"Father, one doesn't just purchase a life's companion like a sack of sugar." Emily shook her head with decision. "I'll find a new dog."

Rev. Brontë and Tabby exchanged worried glances. Emily's stray animals tended to be unpredictable. Her last dog had been rescued from a wild dogfight in front of the church. Emily had given Tabby the fright of her life when she waded into the fray of sharp teeth and flying fur and emerged dragging Grasper by the scruff of his neck. From that day forward, he had been Emily's devoted companion and bared his teeth at everyone else.

"Until you do, perhaps you should carry this." He reached into his wide coat pocket and laid a heavy pistol on the table with a thump. Emily and Tabby stared as it spun round and round. Tabby yelped when it stopped, pointing directly at her. "Tabby, the weapon is only a precaution against anyone with a grudge. It came in very handy last night."

"Father, I don't know how to shoot," Emily said, eyeing the pistol. "But I'm willing to learn." If she were armed then she needn't be afraid of anyone she met on the moors.

He continued, "I will teach you. Someone else in the family should be able to handle a gun, just in case." He touched the corner of his eye and Emily knew he was referring to his clouded vision.

"What about Branwell?" she asked.

"He's an indifferent shot at best," Rev. Brontë said. Emily watched him sympathetically, knowing how desperately he wanted Branwell to be a son he could depend upon. "We'll start this afternoon. You needn't mention this to Charlotte," he said without meeting Emily's eyes.

Emily and Tabby exchanged knowing glances. Prudent Charlotte would never approve of Emily firing a gun.

"It shall be between us," she promised.

He stood up and went to the hook where he kept his long white scarf. He wound it carefully around his neck until he resembled an Elizabethan lady with an enormous ruff. The reverend was particular about his throat and swore by his scarf to keep illness at bay. "After my morning visits I'll set up the target."

Emily's eyes glittered with anticipation. "I'll have the ammunition ready."

Had he been a handsome, heroic-looking
young gentleman, I should not have dared to stand
thus questioning him against his will,
and offering my services unasked.

CHAPTER EIGHT

*P*erfect posture abandoned, Charlotte huddled in the corner of the coach. A month ago—could it only be a month?—she had traversed the same route with Emily. Then Charlotte had had all the confidence, enough to share with Emily. Now she was hurtling across the moors toward a humiliating confession of her failure.

The coach hit a deep rut and Charlotte bounced against the side, bruising her right cheek. It wasn't enough to be sent home in disgrace; she was going to look like a boxer when she arrived.

She called out to the driver, "Go slower, please!" But the coach continued at exactly the same rate of speed, as if even the driver knew her wishes were of no account.

Charlotte had spent every minute of the last two days trying to forget the awful scene in Miss Wooler's office. But she had to face it sooner or later, preferably before she had to explain it to her family. She cringed to think of telling Emily, although Emily was the only one likely to sympathize. How had Charlotte permitted herself to sink so low that Emily was the one with whom she had the most in common?

The summons to Miss Wooler's office had been unexpected. A first-year student had interrupted Charlotte's spelling lesson. When Charlotte tried to demur, the messenger was adamant: Miss Brontë was required immediately.

As Charlotte made her way from classroom to office, she worried perhaps there was bad news from home: Could Emily have had a relapse? Perhaps Father was ill? The autumn was so bad for his sore throats and that silk scarf wasn't warm enough, no matter how many times he wound it about his neck. By the time Charlotte reached the office, she had convinced herself Father was near death and the family on the brink of financial ruin.

So Charlotte had been relieved when Miss Wooler assured her there was no news from home. "I've asked you to come for quite a different reason," she said in a tone so severe Charlotte was instinctively on guard.

Miss Wooler opened her desk drawer and pulled out a tiny handmade book, perhaps three inches square, covered with tiny copperplate handwriting. Charlotte's heart skipped a beat.

"Where did you get that?" she asked before she could stop herself.

"Did you write this . . . this . . ." Miss Wooler asked with a grimace, unable to give the book a proper name. She picked up a large magnifying glass and held it over the book. "*The Romantic Adventures of the Queen of Angria.*"

Charlotte clasped her hands tightly, a denial on her lips.

"Before you answer," Miss Wooler said, "I should tell you this was found in your room."

In a futile attempt to keep her self-respect, Charlotte drew herself up. "I assumed my privacy was respected at Roe Head."

"Not when you are writing—*obscenities.*" Miss Wooler had a hard time saying the word, and when she managed it, she infused the syllables with disdain.

Charlotte gasped and recoiled. "That's not true! My Angria stories are fantasies, nothing more."

"So there are more?" Miss Wooler pursed her lips. "No wonder you haven't been able to concentrate, if your attention is consumed by vulgarity!"

Consumed. What an apt word, Charlotte thought. Lately she had thought of nothing else but her stories. Even getting up in the morning was difficult because the world of Roe Head was not Angria. Her obsession with her fantasy world frightened her.

Charlotte slumped in her chair. "What are you going to do?"

Miss Wooler held up Charlotte's pages by the corner as if she were afraid of contagion. "This is cause enough to dismiss you," she said.

Charlotte gasped; this was worse than she had imagined.

"Or perhaps I should write to your father immediately," Miss Wooler said slowly.

Charlotte felt the blood drain from her face. Father must never know. Ever since she had become the oldest child, she had kept her secrets hidden with handwriting too small for her father to decipher.

"I would if you were still my student," Miss Wooler continued. "But you are my employee, a young woman of nineteen. I am torn between my affection for you and my duty to my students."

Charlotte rushed around the wide desk to kneel at Miss Wooler's feet. Clutching at Miss Wooler's hands, she cried, "Please let me stay. I need this position. I was your best student. I can be your best teacher. . . . If only you'll give me another chance!"

Miss Wooler's sternness softened as she looked down at Charlotte's imploring face. "So you do want to continue here?"

"Yes!" Charlotte let the heartfelt word speak for itself.

"I think you should take some time to consider your situation. Go home for a week or so. If at the end of that time you can assure me you will never contaminate Roe Head School with this filth again, I will take you back."

Suddenly Charlotte was brought back to the present. She heard screaming. For a moment she was afraid her imagination had taken over once again. Then she realized the frightened voice was only too real.

"Help me! Stop, please!"

The carriage jerked to a halt, sending Charlotte to the floor in a heap of skirts and hand luggage. "Driver, what happened?" Charlotte shouted. There was no answer, but she could hear the driver expostulating with a woman.

"What were you thinking, miss? You could have been killed!"

"Help me, please." The woman's voice was ragged, as though she had been screaming for a long time.

Charlotte clambered out of the carriage to see a woman, perhaps in her late forties, dressed in the most makeshift of country dresses, pleading with the driver. Most likely she had come from the moorland track intersecting the road. Her hair was a reddish blond shot through with gray, hanging loose below her shoulders. Charlotte noted the vestiges of what must have been a remarkable prettiness in her youth. Her pale blue eyes were never still, darting from the driver's irate face to the empty track behind and then to Charlotte. Seeing another woman, she cried out in relief and clasped Charlotte's hands. The driver gratefully abandoned the hysterical woman and went to check his horse.

"Won't you help me? I'm desperate." Her hands were soft, Charlotte noticed, unusual in a woman who looked like a farmer's wife. But there were marks about her wrists, making Charlotte wonder if she had been restrained. "I ran away, but it won't be long before they come looking for me."

The woman was quite tall, and Charlotte felt at a disadvantage peering up at her. She noticed that the mysterious woman's pupils were dilated, huge black pools fixed on Charlotte's face.

"What's your name?" Charlotte asked, not committing herself to anything. As a clergyman's daughter, she had often heard terrible stories of husbands beating their wives. Sympathetic as she was, her father had taught her to mind her own business. Neither the law nor the husbands welcomed interference.

"I shan't tell you lest my brute of a . . ."

"Husband?" Charlotte prompted.

"Husband? I wish 'twere my husband. At least when he was alive, I was protected. But now, I am alone." As she spoke, her voice grew louder and shriller.

"You have no one?" Charlotte asked.

"He's taken everything from me: my son, my fortune, and now my freedom." The woman began to sob.

"You mustn't speak so wildly," Charlotte soothed.

"If he catches me, he'll kill me. That would solve all his problems!"

Despite her frenzied manner, Charlotte could tell the mysterious woman did not lack an education. "Madam, be reasonable. I cannot help you if I don't know your name."

"How do I know you won't tell him where I am? Maybe you are in it with him!"

"In what? With whom?" Charlotte interrupted. "Don't be foolish. You stopped my carriage! Now tell me your name, or I'll get on with my journey and leave you behind."

The sound of hooves on the track behind them made them all whirl around. The woman moaned and closed her eyes. A fine-looking gelding galloped up the track, carrying a man of forty years or so. The driver, who had removed himself to a convenient rock, looked up curiously from his tamping of tobacco into his pipe.

The sun was behind the rider, and at first Charlotte could only make out his silhouette. He wore a long coat draped across the horse's hindquarters and his face was in shadow. For a moment, Charlotte saw the duke of Angria, her fictional hero suddenly given weight and heft. She felt her throat close up and shyness overtake her.

As he got closer, the dream quality faded and Charlotte saw he was just a man, although his profile was rather handsome. His dark beard was pointed and gave him a distinguished air. His mouth was closed in a tight angry line and his eyes narrowed when he saw the carriage. When he was close to the crying woman, he reined in his horse. He dismounted and stood very close to her. Suddenly his manner changed and he became the picture of a concerned rescuer. "There you are, Rachel. We've been frantic with worry for you."

"I'm sorry, Robert." Rachel gulped back her tears.

Charlotte immediately noticed his light-blue eyes were just like the mystery woman's. They must be related, she thought. But Rachel had said she had no one.

"The nurse is waiting for you," he said to Rachel. He glanced over at the carriage driver. "If she's done any damage, I'll pay for it."

Charlotte drew herself up. How dare he act as if she were of no importance? "Address me, please," Charlotte said. "I hired the carriage."

He swung round and seemed to see Charlotte for the first time. After a hesitation, he touched his hat. He wore fine leather gloves. "I beg your pardon, miss. But this is no concern of yours."

"She's not well," Charlotte said. "Did you say she has a nurse?"

"I apologize if she delayed your journey," he said brusquely. "She won't be troubling you again."

Charlotte's eyes narrowed; his words sounded innocent enough, but his demeanor worried her.

"May I ask your name, sir?" she asked.

After an awkward pause, he said, "Robert Heaton."

Now she had a name to go with the face, Charlotte realized she had seen him before. "Of Ponden Hall?"

He stiffened as though Charlotte had said something of greater import than his address. He reached out to lock his hand around Rachel's wrist. Rachel, so voluble before, said nothing.

"Yes," he said. "And you are?"

"Miss Charlotte Brontë," Charlotte replied.

"The reverend's daughter?" His eyes shifted uneasily, as though he would have preferred her to be a stranger.

"What is happening here, Mr. Heaton?" Charlotte asked. "Who is this unfortunate lady?" She gestured to Rachel.

"She's a dependent of the family. As you can doubtless see for yourself, she's not right in the head." He gave her a wry smile. "Did she tell you she had enemies and she had to escape them? Perhaps she asked you to hide her?"

Rachel started to speak. "Robert, I didn't mean anything by it." She suddenly closed her mouth. Charlotte saw Rachel's wrist was turning blue under his grip.

"Does she run away often?" Charlotte asked slowly.

He shook his head. "No, she has a devoted servant to look after her, but mad people can be diabolically clever."

"She didn't sound mad to me," Charlotte said, catching her bottom lip between her teeth.

"That's her cunning," he assured her. "An inexperienced young lady like yourself is easily fooled."

Charlotte choked back an angry retort. Before she could recover her voice, he spoke again. "My family's affairs have intruded on your journey long enough."

Rachel spoke before Mr. Heaton could stop her. "Robert, this lady only wanted to help me."

"Hush," he said, making the gentle word sound more like a threat than a reassurance.

Charlotte glanced back to the driver. He was puffing his pipe, uninterested and uninvolved. He would be of no help whatsoever. She didn't trust this Mr. Heaton, but what could she do?

"It is still several miles to Haworth, and Ponden Hall is two miles beyond town," Charlotte said. "Perhaps I can assist you with transportation?"

"That's not necessary," Heaton said. "I'll make sure she's safely home."

"All the way to Ponden Hall?" Charlotte pressed.

He paused. Finally he said, "She's not staying at Ponden Hall. Thank you, Miss Brontë. I apologize for any inconvenience." He bowed slightly and not very gently propelled Rachel toward his horse. With no apparent effort, he lifted her into the saddle and led the gelding down the path without any further word of farewell.

Seeing Charlotte was ready to leave, the driver knocked the ash out of his pipe and held the door open so she could enter the small carriage. "Did she seem mad to you?" Charlotte asked.

"Stark raving mad," he said.

"To me she seemed frightened rather than insane."

"Miss, you're fancying things." He made sure she was settled. "A powerful imagination leads to nothing but trouble." He shut the door and the carriage lurched forward.

"I did wrong to let him take her," Charlotte muttered to herself, her eyes fixed on the backs of the strange pair moving along the track.

I have a place to repair to, which will be a
secure sanctuary from hateful reminiscences,
from unwelcome intrusion—even from
falsehood and slander.

CHAPTER NINE

*I*f Charlotte could have prolonged her homecoming, she would have. She had hidden in the shadows within the carriage the entire last quarter hour to avoid being seen. But eventually the gig pulled up in front of the gray stone parsonage, the last house in town before the moors.

Charlotte usually welcomed the sight of her home. Its symmetry was reassuring, with its center door flanked by two windows on each side and five windows above. Even the narrow front garden, facing the graveyard, was pleasantly familiar. Rising from the end of the churchyard, the church towered over all as though it was sheltering the family home within its shadow.

Charlotte spied Emily coming through the front gate. Her dress hung about her thin frame, and with a sigh Charlotte noticed that she wore only one petticoat at most. Her sister seemed even taller than usual, although that might be from the weight she had lost. Emily's fair hair was loose about her face and there was a bright color in her cheeks. She looked— Charlotte struggled to find the word—happy.

"Emily!" Charlotte cried, jumping out of the carriage to embrace her. Her reservations forgotten, suddenly Charlotte was glad to see her sister, especially looking so well.

"Charlotte!" Emily stood with her arms at her side, dismay in her eyes. No sooner had Aunt B. left than Charlotte arrived unexpectedly to ruin Emily's fun. "What are you doing home?"

"Miss Wooler thought I needed a little rest," Charlotte equivocated.

"In the middle of the term? What about your classes?" Emily asked.

"Are you accusing me of neglecting my duties?" Charlotte shot back.

"Of course not. Charlotte, what's wrong with you?" A thought came into Emily's mind and made her go pale. "Are you ill? Have you been coughing?"

"No, nothing like that," Charlotte said sharply. "And yourself? Are you recovered?"

Emily nodded. "Today is the first day I've been permitted out. I'm going to take full advantage," she said. She opened the gate and stepped out. "I'll see you at supper." Leaving Charlotte slack-jawed with surprise, Emily ran up the path toward the moors.

"Charlotte!" Tabby stood in the front door, drying her hands on a dishtowel. As always, her pale straw-colored hair had escaped from her untidy bun and flew about her face. "We didn't know you were coming home!"

Charlotte went inside, followed by the driver carrying her small valise. She gave him a coin for his trouble.

"I'm only home for a few days, Tabby," Charlotte explained. "Where is Father? And Aunt B.? And Branwell?"

"Well, you've just missed your aunt. She's gone."

"Gone where? She never goes anywhere."

Tabby grinned as though her face would break. "She's off to Scarborough with Anne."

"Amazing," Charlotte said, but inwardly she seethed. Everyone seemed to have adventures but her. "And Father?"

"He was called out to that Mr. Grimes who's always dying, but never dies," Tabby said.

"What about Branwell? I thought he at least would be here." Unspoken was the thought running at the tops of both their minds: Branwell doesn't have anywhere else to be.

Tabby's smile disappeared from her face as though she'd wiped it away with a polishing cloth. "Branwell is visiting some friends."

"Who?"

With a shrug of her ample shoulders, Tabby said, "He's always going to a meeting or someone's house and he won't ever say anything about it." She looked around as if to spy an eavesdropper in the flagstoned hallway. "He's drinking. Ever since he went to that fancy art school in London and returned a scant week later, he's been acting strangely. Your father's worried."

Charlotte followed Tabby into the kitchen. Tabby opened the bin where she kept the vegetables and began to chop celery and onions. Glancing at Charlotte, she said kindly, "I'm sure everyone will be home soon for supper."

"I saw Emily going out," Charlotte said. "She looked healthy." Try as she might, she could hear the bitterness in her own voice. "She's recovered miraculously quickly."

Tabby gave Charlotte a sharp look. "Thank the Lord for that. And thank goodness you were there at school to look after her. She was ever so ill; your father was mortally afeared she was going to die. I've never seen him so fretful."

"Of course he was," Charlotte said.

"None of that green-eyed monster, Miss Charlotte. It doesn't suit you," Tabby scolded. "We would have been just as distressed for you."

"I doubt it," Charlotte muttered, but too low for Tabby to hear over her chopping.

"Sit down, child, and stop fretting no one is here to greet you when you didn't tell them you were coming! How was your journey?"

"It was fine," Charlotte said, settling herself on a stool. "My trip was uneventful until a few miles away from Bradford. Then the oddest thing happened."

She described the woman who had stopped the carriage and how Mr. Robert Heaton had taken her away without so much as a word. "Tabby, you know everyone around here."

Tabby paused in her chopping. "That I do."

"Who was she? Mr. Heaton said she was a dependent of the family."

Tabby paused, as if she had to gather all the details buried deep in her capacious memory. "I've never heard about any dependents. It's not a large family. But Robert Heaton had a sister once." Tabby sighed. "Hers was a tragic story."

Charlotte leaned forward. "Tell me."

"She was a pretty young thing, and bright. Her father sent her to Leeds for school." Tabby shook her head sadly. "It turned out badly."

"What happened to her?"

"A man." Tabby wielded the knife with an angry force that made Charlotte's eyes widen. "Isn't it always? He was the son of a shopkeeper. Not nearly good enough for the only daughter of a landowner like Mr. Heaton. He got the girl into trouble, if you know what I mean."

"Tabby, I'm almost twenty. Of course I know what you mean." But Charlotte felt the blush rise on her cheeks. "What did her family do?"

"What could they do with a babe on the way?" Tabby shrugged. "Mr. Heaton made them marry, of course. But with such a beginning, how could it end well?"

"They were unhappy?" Charlotte asked.

"Her husband drank and spent all the money her father settled on her. I heard she had as many bruises as you have books. When he died a few months later, everyone was happy for her. She came back to Ponden Hall to have her little boy."

"She should have been safe at her father's house," Charlotte said.

"Ah, but the family never let her forget her mistake. Right cruel they were to her. And the boy suffered as well." A tear rolled down Tabby's cheek; whether from the sad story or the onion, Charlotte didn't know.

"That's not fair!" Charlotte said.

"I thought you were a grown lady—you know life is neither fair nor kind." Tabby pushed the chopped vegetables into an iron pan and lit the stove. "It didn't help that the boy was sickly. Mr. Heaton might have forgiven her if his grandson had been a boy to be proud of."

"What was his name?"

"Lawrence, Larry, or maybe Harry? That's right. He was called Harry."

Charlotte knitted her brow. "And he lived at Ponden Hall?" At Tabby's nod, Charlotte said, "We used to visit the library. A most beautiful room. There was a boy there, a little older than us, and pale like a wraith. He always stared at Emily. I never talked to him, but she did."

"That could have been him." Tabby looked up from the simmering vegetables. The smell filled the room and Charlotte felt her stomach rumble from hunger. Tabby went on, "Harry's uncle, Mr. Robert, the one you met today, made his life unbearable until he ran away. And that was the last anyone heard of him. So old Mr. Heaton drove off his only grandson and his son still hasn't taken a wife. And now the old man is dead in his grave."

Charlotte leaned forward. "Robert Heaton is a bachelor?" she asked.

"Don't go setting your cap at him, young lady," Tabby said, shaking the knife at Charlotte. "He's not a good man."

"You're being ridiculous, Tabby," Charlotte exclaimed. "I mistrusted him on sight."

Tabby rolled her eyes.

"What happened to the girl?" Charlotte asked hurriedly.

"I don't recall." Tabby frowned. "I remember hearing she took her son's leaving very hard."

Charlotte asked slowly, "Could the woman I met today been his sister? He called her Rachel. Could she have fallen so far?"

Tabby's eyes glittered with the prospect of a rich tidbit of gossip. "Maybe."

"If it is her," Charlotte mused, "she's afraid of her brother. Something's not right there."

"Well, Miss Charlotte. Remember your father's first rule."

"Don't meddle in parish affairs. I know. It's curious, though, don't you think?"

"I'd rather hear about that school of yours."

Obediently, Charlotte told Tabby all about school, not mincing any words. Tabby laughed and laughed at Charlotte's unkind descriptions of her students. "And you are fed well at school? It's warm enough?"

Charlotte had undergone this catechism upon every return from school. "Of course. Roe Head is not like that other school."

They were both silent, remembering how Maria and Elizabeth had suffered. The cold and damp, combined with the inadequate food, had killed them, of that Charlotte was certain. "I suppose Emily and I should consider ourselves fortunate to have survived," she said quietly.

"The Lord only takes those he needs. You and Emily were spared because you have wonderful futures in front of you."

But didn't her other sisters have wonderful futures, too? Charlotte wondered. She pushed away the blasphemous thought. Glancing out the kitchen window, she saw a flash of unmistakable red hair. Branwell was passing by the house without coming in. Remembering what everyone had said about his erratic behavior, she decided to find out for herself. "How much time do I have before supper?" she asked.

"At least an hour."

"I won't be that long." Charlotte slipped out the back door and ran with light steps around the house to let herself out the front gate. Branwell had disappeared. He might be in the church, she thought, although she was hard-pressed to think of a reason.

Skirting the graveyard, she entered the church. It was empty at this hour; no Branwell. Well, if she couldn't visit with her live brother, she'd spend some time with her dead sisters. Charlotte's feet led her unerringly to the gravestone in the floor.

Staring down, she murmured, "Hello, Elizabeth. I'm back from school. I wanted to let you know I haven't forgotten you and Maria."

The tall church door creaked open and Charlotte fell silent. Emily would happily talk to the dead in front of the whole congregation, but Charlotte was shyer. When footsteps headed toward her, she ducked into a pew box and crouched down. She peeked over the box and saw it was John Brown, her father's sexton for the past ten years. He lived across from the parsonage above his own workshop, digging graves, carving tombstones, and keeping the church in good order. He had a broom and was heading for the vestry when another voice stopped him in his tracks.

"John!" It was her brother's voice.

Charlotte started to get to her feet. How fortuitous! Branwell had found her.

"Worshipful Master!" Branwell called.

Worshipful Master? Charlotte stiffened. Why was Branwell calling Mr. Brown such a ridiculous name? She experienced a sense of unease and stepped back into the shadows of the pew box.

John Brown turned around, scowled, and with a sharp motion drew his finger across his throat.

"I'm sorry. I forgot," Branwell stammered.

John's stern face relaxed. "You're new to our ways. But remember, you are sworn to secrecy."

"Not yet I'm not," Branwell said. Charlotte recognized the touch of sullenness in his voice. "But I want to be."

"Do you have the money?"

Branwell reached into his pocket and pulled out two sovereigns. A fortune for a poor man with no income. Charlotte wondered where he had gotten it. "When will it happen?" Branwell asked.

"Friday."

Branwell's face lit up and abandoned his momentary disgruntlement. "So soon? Finally I'll be one of you!"

"If you survive the ritual," John said with a smile.

Charlotte almost jumped up from the pew to demand what was going to happen to her little brother two days hence. After a moment's reflection, she decided she might learn more if she stayed concealed.

"Where?" Branwell asked, apparently undaunted by the danger.

"Newall Street. At six o'clock. You remember the sign I taught you?"

Branwell started to hold up his fingers in the shape of a *V* but John batted his hand down.

"Idiot! You must be discreet. The price for breaching our secrets is high."

"Of course, of course." Branwell was practically trembling with excitement. "Six o'clock on Friday. Newall Street. I'll be there."

John Brown nodded solemnly and the two parted ways.

From her hiding place, Charlotte was trembling herself with fear for her feckless brother.

"Oh, Branwell, what have you gotten yourself into this time?" she whispered.

CHAPTER TEN

*Y*ou've been home barely a day, Charlotte, and already you're insufferable!" Emily flung Charlotte's list of chores on the floor and folded her arms tightly across her chest. "I managed my chores perfectly well when you were away."

"I thought a schedule of tasks would be useful." Charlotte plucked the hateful paper from the floor and waved it in Emily's direction.

Charlotte's constant need to tidy everything and order everyone about was driving Emily mad. "My dear sister, we all do our share without being told."

"Is that so? It must be pleasant not to have any obligations or responsibilities. No wonder you left school!"

"And why did *you* leave school, Charlotte?" Emily shot back. "That's the *only* subject you've been reticent on."

"I'm going back to Roe Head," Charlotte said. "Which is more than I can say for you. Your illness conveniently brought you home, exactly where you wanted to be."

"That's unkind," Emily retorted. "But surely it was a good thing I left, else I'd be transformed into a miserable tyrant like you!"

"That's a wicked thing to say!"

Emily didn't back down an inch. "I wish you had stayed at Roe Head. The house was a happier place without you in it."

Charlotte recoiled and red patches appeared high on her cheeks. She closed her lips in a tight line and deliberately tore the paper in half. "Are you happy now?" As the pieces fluttered to the floor, she turned and headed for the study door. "I'm going to the kitchen, where my contributions are valued."

"You'll have to go farther than that!" Emily shouted after her. Leaving her shawl behind, she ran out of the front door, through the gate, and onto the path leading to the moors. Let Charlotte make her lists—Emily would do as she pleased.

A stiff breeze whipped her skirt around, pressing it against her legs. That was another thing Charlotte had scolded her about. "It's not proper," Charlotte had said. What rule said Emily must wear at least three petticoats to give the dress some shape? Especially since she would just get them dirty. Emily wasn't bothered; why should Charlotte be?

It was a lovely day. The bright morning sun was blinding across the limitless moor. The sky was a brilliant autumn blue, but in the north Emily could see the gathering of storm clouds on the horizon. She reached the place where two moorland paths intersected. She could go east to her favorite waterfall . . . or west toward Ponden Hall and her mystery man from the other night. Her father's admonitions rang in her ears. But she told herself there couldn't be any danger in full light of day and headed west.

Soon she was a stone's throw from the camp where she had received her scare two nights ago. She did wish she had her father's pistol weighing down her pocket. To her father's surprise, if not her own, Emily had been a good shot. Now that Charlotte was back, who knew how long it would be before she got another lesson?

The campsite was tucked into a fold of a hill and was almost invisible unless you were looking for it. Emily realized she had only found it that night because she had followed the light of the campfire. There was no smoke from a fire now.

In the daylight she could see there was a canvas tent set up in the shadow of the hill. Unless she was mistaken, if she climbed to the top of the hill, she would have an excellent view of Ponden Hall. The shelter would be inadequate in the winter, but until the autumn turned colder, it would protect the occupant from the rain. Just beyond the rock was a small natural spring. It was a good spot to set up camp.

She heard a low snarl. Clutching the stick like a weapon, she advanced into the camp. The huge mastiff whose acquaintance she had made two nights earlier lay on the ground. A chain from his collar twisted around a rock formation to keep him tethered. He lifted his head and panted. His tongue was lolling as though he were desperately thirsty.

Where was the stranger? Scanning the surrounding countryside, Emily edged up to the campsite. The fire was mostly out, but when she poked at the embers with a stick, she saw some were still glowing. Someone had been here recently.

Finding a small bucket by the fire, she dipped it into the small spring. She brought the bucket to the dog's mouth. He was so eager to get his massive snout into the can that he knocked it out of her hands. She grabbed his collar to hold him back. Without warning, he snarled at her and nipped at her arm, drawing blood.

"Ow!" Emily cried. "Why would you do such a thing?" When she looked closer, she saw the leather collar was too tight and had rubbed his skin so badly there was an open sore. "You poor thing! Let me get that off you." Emily unhooked the heavy collar and flung it aside. The chain clinked as it hit the ground. "What kind of devil would lock you up like this?"

Only then did it occur to her the dog might attack. But no, her instincts were sound. His tail thudded even faster than her beating heart and he eyed the water thirstily. She held it firmly on the ground so he could drink it without mishap. She rubbed the top of his bony head with her free hand. Her arm throbbed.

"Boy, you didn't mean to do it. Your master is to blame. And I'll be sure to tell him so if I meet him."

The dog whimpered. He drank deeply, pressing his whole body against her. She thumped him on the side.

"You're a good dog, aren't you? You're a keeper."

He wagged his tail and she grinned. "Keeper? You like that name? Then Keeper you shall be." She cringed to think of what her father would say when she brought the enormous dog home. On the other hand, her father couldn't hope to find a better guard dog. Who would bother her with Keeper at her side?

She dunked her handkerchief in the remaining water and cleaned her arm around the bite. She would have to do something about that when she got home. But for now, she was going to find out about the absentee landlord of this fine estate. She took a long look round to make sure she was truly alone, then ducked under the canvas.

She explored the tidy area. Several blankets were neatly rolled up against the tent wall. There was a small wooden trunk—easily portable. It was irresistible. Without a qualm, Emily tried to lift the latch. It was locked. She examined the lock; it was not a complex one. She pulled out one of the few hairpins still in her untidy hair. With a little poking and manipulation of the tumblers, she managed to open the trunk.

The hairs on the back of her neck rose when she thought of what the owner might say if he found her rummaging through his belongings. Overcoming her scruples, she looked inside.

There was a change of men's clothing. Whoever her mysterious stranger was, he knew about clothes of quality. Beneath the clothes was a cache of newspapers. She picked them up, recognizing the *Leeds Mercury*. Her father subscribed to it, too, often contributing polemical letters to the editor or the occasional poem.

There was the obituary about Mr. Paul Heaton of Ponden Hall. As Emily leafed through the clippings, she noticed they were all about the strife between the millworkers and the owners. But in every newspaper story, the Heaton mills were mentioned, particularly the huge capital improvements in the mills made by Robert Heaton, the heir to the family fortune. Surely the site of the camp, so near to Ponden Hall, was no coincidence.

She dug a little deeper and found several leather-bound books. Hmmm. Byron's *Childe Harold's Pilgrimage*. She hadn't read that in years. In fact, as she recalled, she had been forced to read it secretly at Ponden Hall. Even her father, a liberal in so many respects, had balked at giving Byron to an eleven-year-old.

She opened the book and saw a bookplate from Ponden Hall on the endpaper. So the mystery man had access somehow to the Heaton library.

There was a map of the Haworth Moor—she had never seen one so detailed. It was filled with pen scratches, as though someone was marking off locations. A treasure map perhaps?

But she had never heard the moor had any buried gold—or any wealth at all.

In the farthest corner of the trunk, she found a small box. She pulled it out—it was heavy with a rattling sound inside. She brought it into the light and pursed her lips. She had handled a similar box only yesterday morning. The box contained lead balls for a pistol. With a sense of urgency, she rummaged through everything again, searching for the gun that went with the ammunition.

"What the devil do you think you're doing?" An angry male voice took her breath away. She dropped the lid closed and whirled around.

A tall stranger, his face shadowed by a hat, pointed a gun at her heart. Now she knew where the pistol was.

You looked very much puzzled, Miss Eyre;
and though you are not pretty any more than
I am handsome, yet a puzzled air becomes you.

CHAPTER ELEVEN

*C*harlotte shoved open the kitchen door with both hands, slamming it into the wall.

"Miss Charlotte, gently with the door!" Tabby ordered. She was at the large sink, peeling potatoes. "That wall was just whitewashed and there you go scuffing it. That's not like you."

Charlotte pulled up a stool next to Tabby. "Don't scold me, Tabby. I've just had a blazing row with Emily." She began to arrange the carrots on the table in order of length.

Tabby chuckled. Charlotte's eyes narrowed. "Pray tell, Tabitha, what is so amusing?"

"We've been wondering when you and Emily would have words. Your father thought the peace would last at least another day. I knew better."

"That's outrageous," Charlotte sputtered. "Just because Emily is aggravation personified." She put her elbows on the kitchen table and rested her chin in her hands. Tabby, from long practice, let Charlotte fume in silence. "I don't like being predictable," she complained finally.

Tabby looked up from her peeling. "You and Emily have always struck sparks off each other. I think it is because you are so different."

"Precisely!" Charlotte answered. "Emily is impossible and I'm not!"

A small grin appeared on Tabby's broad face. Her skin, pale like that of so many Yorkshirewomen, was flushed from the heat of the stove.

"I thought everyone would be happy to see me," Charlotte said in a low voice, blinking back tears.

"We are, dear," Tabby said, placing the peeled potato in a pot filled with water.

Charlotte pointed to the potato. "You missed that eye."

The grin disappeared. "I will say, Miss Charlotte," Tabby said, without looking at Charlotte's face as she fished the potato out of the water, "no one complained about my potatoes while you were away."

Grinding her teeth, Charlotte swung her legs down from the stool and stormed out, taking care not to slam the kitchen door on the way out. She thought of visiting with her father, but he was busy in his study and wouldn't welcome any interruptions, even though she had noticed this morning there were cobwebs in the corners above his bookcases. It was on the list of chores Emily had so despised.

She flounced down on the horsehair sofa in the parlor and indulged in a self-pitying moment. "Doesn't anyone want me?" she muttered. She thought of looking for Branwell, but not for very long.

Once, Charlotte and Branwell had been the closest of all the children. He had led their literary adventures and she had gladly followed. But lately he had no interest in reviving their collaboration. She had offered to read his work or show him her own, but he had rejected her every overture. Something was amiss with Branwell, and Charlotte was certain it had to do with his secretive conversations with John Brown.

A large silence filled the parlor as she steeled herself to confront her true grievance. It wasn't dissatisfaction with her family, but with herself. She had nearly lost her job because she could not stop writing at Roe Head. Now she was home, but she had yet to pick up her pen. Instead, she felt the weight of the household on her shoulders. Every dusty corner, unpolished window, or unbeaten carpet haunted her waking moments. Worse was the paralyzing fear that something—an illness or an accident—might take down her father, and then what would happen to them all? If only she could just put aside her cares and write!

There was a knock at the front door. Delighted at the prospect of someone to talk to, Charlotte ran to answer it. She flung open the door and gaped when she saw the sardonic Robert Heaton.

"Good morning," he said.

"Mr. Heaton," she managed to say. Unbidden, he had invaded her thoughts several times in the past few days. Her mental image matched the actual man in every respect. She reexamined him with a critical eye, remembering Tabby's report of his cruelty. But he was no duke of Angria to be banished with a stroke of the pen; he was standing impatiently in her doorway. "What are you doing here?" she asked faintly.

"Miss Brontë," he said, inclining his head. "I'm not accustomed to being left waiting on the step. May I come in?"

Charlotte gulped, stepped back, and opened the door wide for him. As he stooped to enter, she smoothed her skirts and made sure there were no stray strands of hair loose about her face. Despite Tabby's gossip, Mr. Heaton was an important man in her father's parish, she told herself. Besides, only a foolish girl didn't make the most of herself around a marriageable man.

"You are looking very well," he said. "Traveling agrees with so few people, but perhaps you are the exception."

Feeling a warmth in her face, Charlotte managed to say, "I think it is the prospect of being home that puts color in my cheeks." Had she erred by complimenting herself? Would he think she was flirting with him?

He glanced around the entryway and Charlotte tried to see it through his eyes. It was exceedingly plain. For fear of fire, her father wouldn't permit curtains at the windows or rugs on the floor. But she knew it was clean and well-kept. The variety of prints on the wall spoke of a family with wider horizons than the Haworth Parsonage. They were poor, but she wasn't ashamed of her home.

"Please come sit," she said, gesturing to the dining room, which also served as the family parlor. "I will arrange for some tea for us."

He tilted his head to one side and a mocking grin twisted his lips. "I'm sure that would be very pleasant," he said. After a pause, he finished, "However, my business is not with you. I am here to see the reverend."

Charlotte felt as though she had received a body blow. "Of course," she answered. "I meant, if you wait in the parlor, I will fetch him for you." Without waiting to see if he obeyed her suggestion, she stalked away.

In front of her father's room, she closed her eyes and banged her forehead against the door. How could she have been so foolish as to believe the most eligible bachelor in Haworth was coming to visit her? On second thought, Mr. Robert Heaton definitely had a malevolent air. No doubt every awful story Tabby had told about him was the gospel truth.

The door suddenly opened and she fell into her father's arms. He held her at arm's length and stared down at her face.

"I thought I heard a knock," he said. "Charlotte, are you feeling well? You look flushed."

She shook her head, "I'm fine, Father. Mr. Heaton is in the parlor."

His bushy white eyebrows rose high on his head. "Heaton? So now he delivers his ultimatums in person?"

"What do you mean, Father?"

"I haven't seen him since his father's funeral, but we've been battling in the newspaper about the shameful way he is treating his workers at the mill. He threatened to have me dismissed for my radical politics."

"That's absurd," Charlotte said, abandoning her personal humiliation. Underneath her righteous anger, Charlotte felt a frisson of fear: If her father was vulnerable, then the family was at risk. "You are doing your Christian duty. How dare he try to bully you!"

"With a champion like you, my darling Charlotte, I need fear nothing," her father said indulgently. "Have him come in and I'll find out what mischief he's making now."

Charlotte hesitated. "Father, would you mind terribly meeting him in the parlor?"

Rev. Brontë raised his bushy eyebrows. "I usually conduct parish business in here; you know that."

"Just this once?" she implored. "There was a slight misunderstanding when he arrived and . . ."

A twinkle in his clouded eyes, the reverend kissed his daughter on the forehead. "Tabby always says a change is as

good as a rest. But somehow I don't think there will be anything restful about Mr. Heaton's conversation."

"Should I join you, Father?" Charlotte offered.

"The discussion may get heated," he warned.

"Against the two of us, he doesn't stand a chance,"
Charlotte assured him.

Rev. Brontë pulled out two chairs from the dining room
table and arranged them for himself and Charlotte in front of
their guest, who sat on the sofa. The way Heaton kept shift-
ing in his seat made Charlotte suspect he found the sofa as
scratchy as she did. He hadn't removed his gloves; he apparently didn't intend to stay for long.

"Mr. Heaton, what can I do for you?" Rev. Brontë asked.

Heaton glanced from Charlotte's face to her father's and
back again. "Perhaps our business is better discussed privately?"

"Is it about the grievances of your workers or is it a personal matter?" Rev. Brontë asked.

Charlotte started. It had not occurred to her Heaton
might be there to discuss Rachel.

"Of course I'm here about my bullheaded employees,"
Heaton snapped. "I want your blasted—excuse me, Miss
Brontë—your letters to the newspapers to stop. Or, better yet, abandon your position and come round to the owners' side. After all, without our mills, the workers have no
employment at all."

Sticking his finger in his ear and twisting as though his
ears were blocked, the reverend said, "I hope I will always do

my duty as a priest and as a human being. Your treatment of the working men who depend on you is abominable." His voice took on the edge Charlotte associated with his preaching. "When you bring in these new machines that replace two out of every four workers, you take food out of their children's mouths! How would you feel if your own family was so threatened?"

Heaton glared at Charlotte. "Leave my family out of this, reverend. I don't know what your daughter has told you, but my relatives are perfectly safe without your meddling."

The reverend looked puzzled. "What are you talking about?"

Heaton gave Charlotte a sharp look. "It's of no matter. Rev. Brontë, the owners have every right to increase our profits however we wish. If you want me to consider the plight of the families who depend on my mills, you must stop railing against me from your pulpit!"

"I'll stop railing when I see progress." Rev. Brontë stood up. "I have a sermon to prepare, so if you will excuse me? Charlotte, please see our guest out." He left the room with an alacrity that just bordered on rudeness.

Alone with Mr. Heaton, Charlotte's mind was racing. Heaton was obviously relieved Charlotte had not told her father about Rachel, the mysterious woman on the moors. Was she his very own sister? Well, she could confirm that right now. And if he were mortified, then so be it. "Mr. Heaton, I hope your sister is well?"

"Sister?" The look of surprise on his face was delightful, but he soon recovered himself. "Oh, yes, you met her the other day." There was a heavy pause. "I don't recall telling you the nature of our relationship," he said with a probing look. "How did you know?"

Charlotte refused to give him the satisfaction. "One hears things," she said, shrugging. "She is recovered from her . . . adventure?"

"Completely."

Well, that took the conversation precisely nowhere, she thought. "I would like to pay my respects. Where can I find her?" she asked.

"She doesn't like strangers to visit."

"But she and I are acquainted now," Charlotte pressed. "I'd like to be of service to her in her illness."

"Miss Brontë . . ."

"Yes?" Charlotte said sweetly.

"May I speak bluntly?"

"Of course." Now she might hear some truth.

"I'm grateful you didn't mention meeting my sister to your father. It shows a discretion I didn't know a woman was capable of, but I'll thank you to leave it at that. My sister has had a difficult life, and I don't want to expose her to the idle curiosity of strangers."

"My curiosity is anything but idle," Charlotte said. "My family has a Christian duty to care for the unfortunate."

"Not in this case," he said. "The Heaton family takes care of its own. Do not bother my sister or any member of my household." He stood up. "I shall take my leave now; goodbye."

Charlotte rose to let him out but before she put her hand on the doorknob, the door was flung open from the outside. Branwell came in.

"Hello, Charlotte." Branwell saw Heaton in the doorway and stopped cold in his tracks. "You? We're supposed to meet at Newall Street, not here."

Heaton drew his breath in with a hiss. Glancing at Charlotte, he said, "Good day, Miss Brontë." Then, looking at Branwell, his right hand went to his eye and he laid his index finger at the side of his aquiline nose.

Branwell swallowed hard. "Never mind. Good day, Heaton." He tugged on his ear and then placed his thumb on his bottom lip. Without another word, he ran upstairs, leaving Charlotte alone with Heaton.

Charlotte could see some sort of secret communication had just passed between Heaton and her brother. But she had the measure of this man and knew better than to ask for details. He would not tell her.

"You know my brother?" Charlotte inquired.

"We're acquaintances," Heaton said, as though the odd scene with Branwell had never taken place. "As I was saying before we were interrupted, please respect my wishes and don't meddle with my sister's well-being." Without waiting for her answer, he left.

Charlotte stood in the doorway, watching his figure go up the path toward the moors and Ponden Hall. She bit her thumbnail and said to his retreating back, "In my own home, no one tells me what to do."

CHAPTER TWELVE

*E*mily's whole world shrank to the round opening of the pistol pointing at her heart. Her entire body clenched against the anticipated impact of a bullet. The mastiff, Keeper, pressed his body against her leg and growled at the man.

"Who are you?" the man holding the gun repeated angrily. He peered into the dim light under the canvas, trying to see her clearly. "And what have you done to my dog?"

"I won't say anything with a gun pointed at me," Emily said, with a composure she did not feel.

Once he heard her voice, the gun wavered in his hand. "You're not a Gypsy," he said. "You sound like a lady."

"But you, sir, cannot claim to be a gentleman until you put that gun away."

The stranger slowly lowered his arm. "I beg your pardon," he mumbled. "I didn't mean to frighten you."

Exulting that even though she was clearly in the wrong, the stranger was apologizing to her, Emily studied him more closely. He was tall, with dark wavy hair and blue eyes that reminded her of cornflowers. To her surprise, he was not much older than she; perhaps he was nineteen or twenty. His features were roughened by wind and sun, but his lips were finely shaped, even when pursed in confusion. He seemed oddly familiar. But how? She rarely met young men.

"You've had a good look at me," he said finally. "Now, tell me who you are and why you're pawing through my things."

"I'm not sure I want to talk with a man who abuses animals and terrorizes young women."

He frowned. "I've never abused an animal in my life."

Emily couldn't help but nod her approval of his priorities. She, too, would put a dog's welfare ahead of a girl's. "He had no food or water. I'd call that abuse, wouldn't you?"

The man ducked under the canvas door and strode over to the rocks by the campfire. Emily followed, grateful to escape the confined space. The man held up a bowl, slick with moisture, that had been turned over. "I left him water, but he's excitable and knocks it over often as not."

"Oh." Her hand dropped to Keeper's head and massaged the knobs on his skull. "But why was he tied up?"

"I've had an intruder," he said, not noticing Emily's instinctive flinch. "But as you can see, he's a terrible watchdog."

"His collar was too small," Emily accused.

"Because he's growing so fast. I ordered a new one last week." A genial smile appeared on his face; Emily liked the way it made his eyes crinkle. "Is the inquisition over?"

"For now," Emily said begrudgingly. The bite wound on her arm ached as though to punish her for misjudging the man. "Will you put away that gun?"

"In return, you must tell me why you are searching my things." He put the pistol in his pocket. "Why don't you sit down? I suspect it may be a long story." He indicated a rock.

"Thank you," Emily said, perching on the rock and tucking her skirt behind her knees. Keeper settled down next to her feet. "You've not told me your name."

"Nor have you. Perhaps when we trust each other more," he said. He knelt by the campfire and added bits of wood until he had a brightly burning fire.

Rather than explain herself, she decided to take the offensive. "Why are you spying on Ponden Hall?"

He started. "I don't know what you mean," he said unconvincingly.

"It's a coincidence that your camp is situated on the edge of Heaton land, near a rise from which you can watch Ponden Hall unobserved?"

He said nothing.

"I wager if we went up to the top of that hill, we'd find signs you have spent time there." She began to get to her feet. "Shall we look?"

"Never mind," he said holding up his palm. "So I've been watching the house." He sat on a rock on the opposite side of the fire and cracked his knuckles.

The gesture wakened a glimmer of recognition in Emily. "Have we met before?" she asked.

"It doesn't seem likely."

Emily stared intently at his face; his sky-blue eyes under dark eyebrows struck a chord in her memory. "Do you prefer the novels of Sir Walter Scott or Lord Byron?" she asked suddenly.

He burst out laughing. "When I was a boy, I loved Scott. But now . . ."

Emily hopped up and ran to the wooden box in the canvas tent. She found the Byron book and brought it back. He narrowed his eyes and held out his hand, but she didn't give it to him. She opened it to the flyleaf.

Hareton Smith
Ponden Hall
1825

"When I was ten or so, I used to visit the library at Ponden Hall," Emily said, watching him closely. "There was a boy I used to see there. Sickly, so more often found in the library than in the fields or stables. His name was Harry. He used to help me get books that were out of my reach."

A slow smile appeared on his face and he said with a reminiscent air, "I recall a scrawny girl with flyaway hair who liked all my favorite books. She was always a curious thing. I suppose that hasn't changed," he said. "It's a pleasure to renew our acquaintance, Miss Brontë."

With a wide gesture to their informal surroundings, Emily said, "Why don't you call me Emily and I'll call you Harry."

He nodded, a wary look in his eyes casting a shadow over his smile.

"One day you were gone. I never heard what happened to you," Emily said. "And now I happen upon you here, not staying in your family home, but lurking around outside like a criminal."

"Perhaps I've become a thief," he said.

"I doubt that," Emily said. "You don't seem in any need. And surely there are easier places to burgle than Ponden Hall, which is always filled with servants and family." She stopped, realizing perhaps the parsonage might be one of those places. The strange events on the moors coincided with Harry's arrival.

She gave herself a little shake and returned to her questions. "Family! Does your family know you are back?"

"No." His tone made it clear it was an unwelcome subject. "Nor do I wish them to."

"Then why are you here?" Emily asked.

"I've come back to reclaim someone who is mine." He was tense, and Emily admired how his whole body seemed focused on his internal purpose. No longer a pale and sickly adolescent, Harry had grown into a fine man with an admirable physique; a hero worthy of inclusion in one of her stories.

"A woman," she guessed, breathless.

"Only the kindest, most wonderful woman in the world," he said, a look of tenderness transforming his demeanor. "I speak of my mother."

Emily blinked. "Your mother?"

"She has suffered such trials and I've been nothing but a misery to her. I'm here to make amends."

"I don't recall your mother," Emily mused. "But your grand-father was important in my father's church. He was a deacon. My father buried him last month." Slowly, remembering the newspaper clippings, she added, "But you know that already."

Harry leapt up and began pacing with wide angry steps. Keeper, at Emily's feet, watched intently, growling deep in his throat. "My grandfather was a brute who would as soon knock me down as look at me. He despised my mother for making a poor marriage and me for being born. I shouldn't have left her here alone, but I thought he might kill me if I stayed."

Emily paid little attention to gossip in the parish. Only the most lurid of her father's dinnertime stories stuck in her mind.

But she had never heard anything scandalous about the Hea-tons until the old man's funeral. Her hand caressing Keeper's shoulder, Emily asked, "And now?"

"Now Grandfather's dead and I want to rescue my mother."

Emily watched him pace, her eyes glistening. A quest. She loved nothing better. "Tell me more," she said.

"I've been at sea these past six years and I've heard noth-ing of her. She's not at Ponden Hall. Even my old nanny, Hannah, is gone. I'm afraid she might be dead."

"Surely it isn't hard to find out," Emily said.

"I don't want to reveal myself to my uncle." He held out his hands in a helpless gesture. "But unless I come into town, how can I find out if she is alive or dead?"

"I can look in the parish records if you like," Emily offered.

After a long speculative look, Harry nodded. "I would be grateful, but please, be careful. My mother's fate depends on your discretion."

Emily's startled gray eyes met his. "Assuming she's alive, you think she is in danger?"

Harry said. "My Uncle Robert is a vicious man. The improvements he's making to the mills must be taking all the money he inherited from his father. My mother's share may be too tempting for him. That's why I have to find her."

"Don't the Heatons own property all over the moor?" Emily asked, thinking of his well-thumbed map.

"Exactly. Robert may have stashed her anywhere."

"What will you do if you find her?" she asked.

"When I find her," he said, "I'll take her far from here. Robert can't be trusted. I've made enough money to support her, even if he has taken hers. She can start life anew."

There was a roll of distant thunder. Both Harry and Emily had been raised on the moors and knew how quickly a storm could overtake them.

"You should get home," Harry said.

"I'll come back tomorrow and tell you what I've learned." As Emily turned to leave, Keeper got to his feet and began to follow her.

"Roland, Roland, get back here, boy!" He called after the mastiff, but the dog didn't respond. "Emily—that's my dog!"

"Dogs choose their own owners." Emily shrugged.

"Perhaps in your imagination," Harry protested. "In the real world, I paid three guineas for that animal."

"Then you should have been a better friend to him." She saw him draw breath to argue and held up her hand. "I accept your explanation that you were trying to be a good master— but apparently he has not."

Harry glanced from the dog to Emily and back again. "Fine. I'll lend him to you. To keep you safe on the moors. But I will expect his return."

"The only danger I've seen on the moors is you," Emily said. "I'll take good care of him." She started for home, Keeper at her heels. She was well satisfied to have learned so much while admitting nothing. She glanced back; he was still watching her.

It little mattered whether my curiosity irritated him;
I knew the pleasure of vexing and soothing him by
turns; it was one I chiefly delighted in, and a sure
instinct always prevented me from going too far.

CHAPTER THIRTEEN

*R*ushing down the hill at her usual headlong pace, Keeper easily matching her, she saw Charlotte pruning the family's sickly lilacs in the garden. Privately, Emily thought the flowers were so spindly they couldn't afford to lose any foliage.

Charlotte noticed her at the gate. "Where have you been?" Her sharp voice reminded Emily they had parted in anger.

"On the moors," Emily said matter-of-factly. "And look what I found." She opened the garden gate and Keeper bounded through.

Charlotte took one look at the huge tawny animal and ran into the house. Through a crack in the door she berated Emily, "Where did you find that awful beast?"

"He found *me*," Emily replied. "His name is Keeper." She pushed open the door and brushed past Charlotte on her way to the kitchen. Charlotte pressed herself against the wall as Keeper walked by, his toenails clicking on the sandstone floor.

In the kitchen, Emily poked the banked fire in the stove until she had coaxed a bit of flame. The kitchen was empty, but Emily knew it wouldn't remain so for long. Without delay, she took a narrow flatiron from its hook on the wall and thrust it into the flame. While it heated, she unwrapped her arm and bathed the place where Keeper had broken the skin with his long teeth.

As though Keeper knew he was responsible, he lay on the floor and pressed his massive head on his paws.

"Don't be ashamed, Keeper," Emily reassured him. "You were only doing your duty." She pulled the iron out of the fire. It glowed a dull red. "This is going to hurt, but it's the only way to make sure I don't get rabies." She took a deep breath and brought the iron to her skin.

She bit her lip to keep from crying out. Keeper smelled the burning flesh and growled. At that moment, Charlotte walked into the kitchen.

"Emily!" Charlotte pulled the iron off Emily's arm. Bits of skin stuck to the hot metal. "Are you deranged?" she snapped as she tossed the iron into the bucket of water kept near the stove in case of fire. There was a long hiss.

"Charlotte, there's no need for hysterics," Emily said, stepping back to avoid the billowing steam. "I'm fine." The tears streaming down Emily's face belied her calm tone. She held her arm stiffly at her side. The dog pressed against Emily's leg, growling at Charlotte.

"Call off the dog, Emily," Charlotte ordered. In the drawer where Tabby kept them, she found a clean cloth and frantically pumped cold water on it until it was soaked through. Turning to her sister, she wrapped the cool cloth around the burn. "It's already blistering, you idiot. What on earth were you doing?"

"I was bitten," Emily said, matter-of-factly.

"I told you it was an awful beast." Charlotte scowled at Keeper. "I'll fetch the doctor."

"I've already cauterized the wound," Emily protested. "There's no need for a doctor."

Charlotte shook her head and opened her mouth to argue.

"Charlotte, please. I don't want to worry anyone. I'm fine."

Narrowing her eyes, Charlotte said, "When you start foaming at the mouth, then may I summon Doctor Bennett?"

"If I start to foam, then it will be too late," Emily pointed out. "And I don't have any faith in doctors anyway."

Charlotte couldn't blame her. There had been too many illnesses in the Brontë family for which the doctors had proven useless.

"If I see any symptoms, I'm sending for him," Charlotte insisted. "But that dog should be put down."

"He's my pet now." Emily dropped her hand lightly on Keeper's head. "Keeper, meet Charlotte."

Charlotte threw up her hands. "I give up. You're absolutely impossible." As she left the kitchen she collided with Branwell in the narrow hallway.

"Charlotte, what is all this noise? I'm trying to work!" he said, a whining tone in his voice.

"You're working?" she said eagerly. "A new Angria story? Can I see it?"

"I've no time for our childish stories," he said. "I am a grown man doing serious work now."

Charlotte recoiled. It was one thing for him to have new friends and be mysterious about his comings and goings, but to abandon Angria was the deepest betrayal of all. "And what kind of work is that?" she asked with a waspish tone.

"None of your concern. While you've been locked in that girls' school, I've become accustomed to my privacy." He threw his head back and his thick red hair framed his face like a halo on fire. "I'll thank you to respect it now that you're back. Or else."

"Or else what exactly?" she asked. And to make certain he paid attention, she held up her fingers in the same twisted way that Mr. Heaton had signaled to Branwell.

Now it was his turn to step back. "You mustn't do that. . . . Girls aren't allowed. . . ."

Charlotte laughed with delight at the success of her little experiment. "Branwell, I'm going to find out all about it, so you might as well tell me now. You never could keep a secret. Tell me about the meeting on Newall Street."

Branwell grabbed her wrist. "I'm warning you, Charlotte, don't meddle." His whisper was full of menace. "You are playing with forces you do not understand." He shoved her against the wall and stormed up the back stairs to his room.

"You're the second person this week warning me not to meddle," Charlotte muttered as she stared after his retreating figure. "But neither of you can keep me from finding out what I want to know." She pulled her shawl off its hook and headed for the door.

"Where are you going?" Emily stood in the kitchen doorway, holding the cloth to her arm.

"Newall Street," Charlotte answered.

"What's on Newall Street?"

Ignoring Emily's question, Charlotte asked, "How long has Branwell been so strange and nervous?"

"When *hasn't* Branwell been excitable?" Emily shrugged. "I don't pay much attention."

"You never do, do you?" Charlotte spat the words. "The whole family could be on the road to damnation and you wouldn't deign to notice." She turned to go out the front door.

"Charlotte, that was uncalled for!" Emily was more confused than angry by Charlotte's outburst.

Charlotte took a deep breath. "You're right, Em. I apologize. Now will you please lie down and rest?" With a hint of a smile she added, "Or will you refuse simply because I suggested it?"

"I'm not as contrary as that," Emily said with a sniff. "I'll consider resting."

"Thank you."

Outside on the front steps, Charlotte peered at the sky. Thick, dark clouds were rolling down from the moors and the first drops of rain were splattering the gravestones in front of the parsonage.

Charlotte hurried down the lane and turned onto Main Street. The church was perched at the top of a steep hill, paved with uneven stones. She picked her way carefully across the gutter running with human waste and dirty water. She rarely ventured into town because the smell was so awful. Thankfully the parsonage had a private privy and its own well, but the rest of the town shared sanitary facilities. Her father, who was always writing to the authorities about better sanitation, had told her once that twenty-four families on one street shared a single privy.

She passed the Black Bull Tavern. The door to the pub opened and a man, smelling of stale beer and sawdust, came stumbling out, nearly knocking her down. She pushed him away and continued farther down the hill to where Main Street intersected Newall Street. The town's only stationer was on the corner. It was just past four o'clock and it was still open.

She pushed open the door, setting a little bell to tinkling. The shopkeeper who emerged from the back was a little man, not much taller than Charlotte. His bald skull had a huge purple birthmark on it like an ink stain. Emily always said it was appropriate for a stationer.

"Hello, Mr. Greenwood."

"Miss Brontë," he said. He tended not to look his customers in the face, preferring to stare at the scratched wood counter. "I heard you were back from school."

"I've been back for a few days," Charlotte said.

"Isn't it the middle of the term?" he asked.

"Yes," Charlotte said curtly. Did everyone know the school schedule?

"What can I get you?" He began to fiddle with a carefully stacked pyramid of ink bottles. "I must say, I hope you don't need more writing paper already. Last time I had to walk to Keighley to supply Miss Emily's requirements."

"That's six miles there and back!" Charlotte raised her eyebrows. Then she realized the import of what he had said. Emily was writing well enough to run out of paper.

"Miss Emily is such a good customer, I'm happy to go the extra mile." He chuckled at his own joke.

"I'm sure she appreciates that," Charlotte said dryly. More likely, she thought to herself, Emily hasn't given it a second thought.

"I saw your sister on the moors a few days ago," Mr. Greenwood said. "Her expression was . . . exalted!"

Charlotte sighed. It was always Emily. "Mr. Greenwood, I need a penknife. I left mine at school."

"Of course." He brought one out. "I'll charge your account?"

"Thank you," Charlotte said, and then arrived at her true reason for coming. "Do you see your neighbors on Newall Street often? What are they like?"

He glanced toward the window. "There's only one. And it's a private club. They don't welcome strangers."

"Isn't there some sort of gathering here on Friday evenings?" Charlotte remembered every detail John Brown had told Branwell.

Mr. Greenwood's hand jerked, knocking over the stack of ink bottles. "I don't know anything about those."

"Your shop is right next door," she persisted. "You must know something."

Greenwood looked directly at Charlotte. "Miss Brontë, you shouldn't be asking questions about them."

Charlotte started. "About whom?"

But try as she might, Charlotte couldn't get any further information out of him. He practically pushed her out of the store. She could hear the lock turning, then she saw the blinds being pulled down.

Her resolve strengthened by the stationer's reticence, Charlotte walked to the only other house on the street. A steep staircase led to a white door. Charlotte noticed the doorknob and knocker were well polished.

After a moment's hesitation, she lifted the knocker. No one answered. She pushed against the door and found it was locked.

Glancing about the alley, she climbed down the stairs and found another entrance on the side leading to the basement of the building. That door was also latched. Charlotte was tempted to give up and go home. But then the thought occurred: What would Emily do?

Charlotte took a closer look at the door. It was loose in its frame, secured only with a hook and eye. She took her new knife and slid it between the door and the jamb, lifting the hook out of its eye. Branwell had taught her that trick. Wouldn't he be surprised she had used it to unearth his secrets? Perhaps when he found out how clever she had been, he would admit her back into his confidence.

She slipped into the tiny storeroom and then carefully closed the door behind her, replacing the hook. "Hello?" she called out. "Is anyone there?" Silence.

She climbed a set of rickety stairs, lit only by a dingy skylight high above her head. It led to a red door with a gold filigree design depicting stonecutters' tools.

She pushed open the door, wincing at the loud creak, and stepped into a long room spanning the length of the building.

Charlotte had never seen a room like it. A table, not unlike an altar, flanked by globes and decorated with strange symbols like pyramids and eyes picked out in gold or stone, stood at the far edge. Heavy floor-length velvet curtains hung at the windows. The paneling was dark, and there were portraits hanging on the walls.

She examined them carefully, recognizing men from her father's parish. They were all men of substance. The very first painting was a flattering portrait of John Brown. He was portrayed facing down a storm, unafraid. The painter's style looked familiar, and she wasn't surprised to see her brother's signature in the corner.

What was Branwell's involvement in this secret room? What would Father say?

A large, ornate trunk was in the corner. She tried to lift the lid. At first she thought it was locked, but then she noticed the latch on the front. It was the kind that would lock when the lid was shut, but to open it all she had to do was move a tab.

Feeling like someone about to discover something shocking—a treasure or a corpse—she opened the trunk. It was full of a dozen or so white aprons. She rummaged through them; they had an odd, skinlike feel that made her shiver. Lambskin, she decided. Next she found a dark blue length of rope, tied into a wide noose, with decorative tasseled ends. Putting that aside, she lifted out a blindfold. Then a compass with a sharp needle such as a sailor would use to anchor the compass to a ship railing. Next, she found a pair of men's cotton pants, the kind her brother might wear to sleep in. She picked this up with her fingertips. They were clean, at least. Lastly she found a length of velvet of the same color and weight as the curtains. What an odd assortment of items!

There was a roll of thunder outside and she drew aside the heavy curtain to check on the weather. Robert Heaton was turning the corner into the alley. She pulled back from the window just in time to avoid being seen. She looked at the watch hanging on a chain around her neck. It was only five o'clock—they were early!

Hurriedly she opened the red door to make her escape, but quickly closed it again when she heard voices in the basement.

She didn't have much time. The trunk was her only option. She examined it carefully. From the inside, she would not be able to open it. She grabbed one of the chisels lying about the room and wedged it near the hinge, climbed inside, and closed the lid over her head. The chisel prevented it from shutting all the way. She had about an inch to see and hear through, and to breathe. It would have to be enough.

No sooner had she secreted herself at the very bottom of the trunk under the fabric than she heard voices outside the room. The door creaked open. Charlotte made herself as still as she could and tried to quiet her pounding heart.

My heart beat thick, my head grew hot; a sound
filled my ears, which I deemed the rushing of
wings; something seemed near me; I was oppressed,
suffocated: endurance broke down; I rushed to the
door and shook the lock in desperate effort.

CHAPTER FOURTEEN

*C*harlotte listened intently, but she couldn't make out anything but indistinct voices in the next room. Buried under the
folds of cloth, the air became hot and stale. From her heels to
the top of her head, there was scarcely an inch of clearance. It
was altogether too reminiscent of a custom-made coffin.

A thin bar of light was visible where the lid was propped
open and she kept her eyes fixed on it. The creak of the door
opening made her start.

"Get the aprons," a raspy voice said. The speaker came
toward her, his hobnailed boots echoing in the empty room.
"And don't forget there's an initiation today."

Hurriedly, Charlotte tried to burrow even deeper under the velvet drapery. She had no idea if she were visible. Suddenly a second voice was at the chair at the end of the chest by Charlotte's head.

He threw open the chest and Charlotte tried to make herself as flat as possible. An overwhelming scent of garlic emanated from him in waves as his hands reached in and pulled out the aprons heaped on top of her. The lightening of weight wasn't a relief but a reminder of how vulnerable she was.

The raspy voice said, "Do you have the compass and the rope?"

Charlotte willed herself not to flinch as his hands searched around the chest. "Here they are," the other voice said. With a snigger, he added, "I've got the pants, too." The chest lid slammed down, but didn't lock because of her forethought to place a chisel in the hinge.

Charlotte breathed again. Cautiously, she peeked out to see the curtains had been drawn and the sliver of light became brighter as candelabras were lit. A thick, sweet smell of incense penetrated her hiding place. She pinched her nose closed to keep from sneezing.

There was a long silence, then after a few minutes, the room filled with men speaking in hushed tones. Not unlike church, Charlotte thought irreverently. Two men moved to the corner where her hiding place was, as though they wanted to speak privately.

"So, Brother, is the Initiate ready?" Charlotte knew that voice from a thousand encounters; it was John Brown. So Charlotte had been right to suspect that odd conversation between Branwell and Brown a few days earlier.

"Yes, Worshipful Master." Although the title was deferential, Charlotte thought the tone was not. Whoever was speaking did not perceive himself to be inferior to Brown, Worshipful Master or not. Charlotte was practically certain the speaker was none other than the prideful Robert Heaton. "I've catechized him thoroughly. He will be fine during the ceremony."

"We are moving too quickly with this one," Brown said. "I've known him most of his life, and he's never been constant to anything for more than a few months."

"Master, only he can do what I need to be done," Heaton insisted.

"I don't like the Three Graces Lodge being involved in your family's business."

"With the Initiate's help we can right an old mistake," Heaton replied. "And the lodge will profit handsomely. Think of the alms the lodge can distribute with my generosity."

Reluctance in his voice, Brown said, "Then let us begin."

What followed next felt like a dream to Charlotte. She heard John Brown—or, as he was ridiculously called, the Worshipful Master—call the meeting to order. Then Heaton announced there was an Initiate petitioning for entry into the Three Graces Masonic Lodge.

The Freemasons! This explained the secrecy. The fraternity was notoriously private. They claimed their purpose was to do good works, but no one, excepting their members, knew anything about their meetings and customs.

"Has any objection been urged against the Initiate?" the Master went on. There was no objection and he called for a ballot to be cast by each Brother.

Charlotte gingerly peeked through the crack between the lid and chest. Each man was handed a black ball and a white one. Then Heaton moved about the room with a box. Each member deposited only one ball. When everyone had voted, he displayed the box for all to see. Every ball was white.

"He is accepted," the Master pronounced. "Bring him hither."

At the door, there were three loud knocks. One of the Brethren, at the Master's signal, responded with three knocks. Outside there was a single knock, which was answered by one knock. The door was opened, and the man with the raspy voice asked, "Who comes there? Who comes there? Who comes there?"

"A poor, blind Initiate, who has long been desirous of having and receiving a part of the rights and benefits of this worshipful lodge."

Charlotte felt as though all the blood had drained from her body. The voice was beloved and familiar. Branwell was the Initiate.

She twisted in the chest and lifted the lid several inches higher to see. Branwell was blindfolded and the length of blue rope hung around his neck and left shoulder. His left foot was bare and his right was in a slipper. He looked small and pale, like a plucked chicken, surrounded by older men wearing lambskin aprons over their suits.

Heaton approached him and pressed the point of a compass against Branwell's bare chest. Branwell yelped in pain and Charlotte clapped her hands over her mouth to keep from crying out.

"Did you feel anything?" Heaton asked.

Through gritted teeth, Branwell answered, "I did."

"That was a torture to your flesh. So may it be to your mind, if ever you should reveal the secrets of Masonry."

Then Heaton grabbed the rope in his fist, tightening it. "Do you feel the rope around your neck?"

Branwell's body tensed, and Charlotte could hear the wariness in his voice. "I do."

"This rope binds you to the Brethren. As we are bound to you. Do you agree to go to the aid of any Brother with all your power?"

"I do," Branwell responded. Charlotte wondered if anyone else heard the relief in Branwell's voice when Heaton released the noose. Heaton pushed Branwell to kneel on the floor.

The Master approached and said, "Mr. Brontë, you are ready to take the solemn oath of an Apprentice Mason. Say after me: 'I, Branwell Brontë, of my own free will in presence of Almighty God, and this worshipful Lodge of Free and Accepted Masons . . .'"

In a quivering yet oddly triumphant voice, Branwell repeated the words. "Do most solemnly swear, that I never reveal the mysteries of ancient Free Masonry, to any person in the known world. Furthermore, I will not write, print, stamp, stain, hew, cut, carve, indent, paint, or engrave it on anything moveable or immoveable, under the whole canopy of heaven, whereby the secrets of Masonry may be unlawfully obtained through my unworthiness."

If the oath hadn't been so frightening, Charlotte might have admired their thoroughness. These fellows didn't leave anything to chance.

Branwell finished in a ringing voice Charlotte barely recognized: "I do most solemnly swear, binding myself under no less penalty than to have my throat cut across and my tongue torn out by the roots, so help me God."

Charlotte all at once saw her danger—and, worse, Branwell's. If she were discovered, both their lives were forfeit. Her infernal curiosity had put them both in danger. She must stay concealed. She lowered the lid and carefully arranged the cloth to hide her from anything but the most determined inspection of the chest.

She could hardly hear the rest of the ceremony. But then the Worshipful Master's voice suddenly rang out. "Brethren, bring this new-made brother from darkness to light."

Charlotte started when the floor resounded with an enormous thump. The Brethren were clapping and stomping their feet.

"Remove the blindfold and we will dress you appropriately."

Charlotte, huddled under fabric, could only imagine what Branwell looked like—the bandage dropping from his eyes. He would be blinking furiously, giving him the look of a weeks-old kitten.

The Master was saying, "Brother Branwell, I now present you with a lambskin apron, an emblem of innocence, and the badge of a Mason; it has been worn by kings, princes, and potentates of the earth, who have never been ashamed to wear it."

Heaton's authoritative voice said, "Brother, I present you with the working tools of an Apprentice Mason, a chisel and a square."

Branwell murmured something Charlotte couldn't quite catch.

Heaton concluded by saying, "Brother, it has been a custom to demand from a newly made brother, something of a metallic kind, that it may be deposited in the archives of the lodge, as a memorial that you were herein made a Mason."

"I have two guineas!" Branwell shouted.

Charlotte pursed her lips. She knew very well where that money came from. Her father, who said he could not afford to buy her a new dress, handed out sovereigns to Branwell as though they were trifles.

Finally, the initiation ended. Charlotte, feeling a little drowsy from the lack of fresh air, heard Branwell being congratulated by his new brethren. The meeting became more of a social gathering, with men talking in small groups. She became more alert when she heard Robert Heaton's voice.

"Brother Branwell, welcome," he said.

"Thank you, Master Heaton," Branwell said ingratiatingly. "I will be more than happy to help you with that little family problem . . . now we are lodge brothers." He lowered his voice and Charlotte had to strain her ears to hear him. "I've been practicing all week."

"Good man!" A slapping noise, as though Heaton had clapped Brandon on the back. "How soon can you do it?"

"This very night," Branwell answered, "if I have the opportunity." They moved away from the chest.

Oh, Branwell, Charlotte thought, what nefarious plot have these Masons drawn you in to? She heard nothing else of interest and finally dozed off. When she awoke, the room was almost silent. Had they all left? But no, she heard the same hobnailed boots from before.

"Be sure to put everything back the way it ought," the raspy voice said.

Charlotte heard steps close to her chest and the creak of the lid being opened. The man who smelled of garlic. She nearly cried out when a great weight descended upon her head. It was the lambskin aprons; their heat and stink was suffocating her.

"The chest isn't closing properly," the garlicky man said. Charlotte felt rather than saw his presence leaning over the chest. "Blimey, a chisel got stuck in the hinge."

"Careless," said the other.

"I've taken care of it. No harm done."

The lid to the chest slammed shut, locking itself with a loud and final click.

CHAPTER FIFTEEN

Outside, the rain cleansed the filth from the streets and washed the grime off the gravestones. Emily sat alone in the parlor, oblivious to the weather. Her pen moved frantically, as though her words were like water overflowing its channel. She wrote of a strange man hiding on the moors, his only companion a fierce mongrel dog. She thought mongrel sounded better than a purebred mastiff. The man had been wronged and yet his heart remained virtuous. Or perhaps he was vindictive, bent on avenging his rotten childhood, but a chance encounter with a young woman led to his redemption. She stared at an inkblot on the paper and weighed her options. The story could go either way.

Every few minutes, she would leap to her feet and circle the dining table, round and round, before flinging herself back into her chair to write again.

"Miss Emily!" A shout made her pen slip across the page. With a half-expressed curse, she looked up to see Tabby in the doorway holding a dinner tray.

"Tabby! Don't scare me like that!"

Unperturbed, Tabby deposited the tray on the table. "You didn't hear me the first three times I spoke." She straightened out the papers, removing the last half-filled sheet forcibly from Emily's hands. "I've fed your father in his study, but I can't find Branwell or Charlotte." She gasped as she caught sight of Keeper, whose massive body was longer than the hearth in front of the fireplace.

Stepping back toward the safety of the door, Tabby asked, "You found a new dog?" Her expression begged Emily to say no.

Emily nodded. The defiant tilt to her chin warned Tabby not to argue.

But Tabby said only, "He'll eat us out of house and home."

"He's a wonderful guard dog," Emily countered, shoving the steaming stew in her mouth. "You've been worried that we'll all be killed in our beds. Not with him about." She noticed Tabby wore her shawl. "Where are you going?" she asked around the chunks of mutton burning her tongue.

"It's my day out tomorrow, and the reverend has given me leave to stay the night with my sister in town. But I can't leave until I've given Charlotte her dinner; do you know where she is?"

Emily could see Tabby was eager to be gone. "I expect she's with Branwell." Emily shrugged. "I'll make sure she eats when she returns. Go."

"I'm glad Charlotte has made her peace with Branwell. She's been out of sorts since she came home. Maybe they'll start their scribbling again and we'll get some peace."

"It isn't scribbling, dear Tabby. Writing is what makes life sweet to the tongue. Charlotte will start to write again soon, whether or not Branwell is amenable. She won't be able to stay away." Emily jumped up and kissed Tabby on the cheek. "Have a lovely visit with your sister."

Briefly, Emily wondered where Charlotte might be, but decided it was none of her affair. If Emily wanted her own privacy, she could hardly intrude on Charlotte's.

Emily picked up her pen again. It seemed like only a moment later before her father interrupted her writing. She looked up, confused because the room was so dark. Night had fallen while she was working.

"You must save your eyes, my dear," he said, lighting a candle for her.

"It's Charlotte and Branwell whose eyes are weak—mine are fine."

"All the more reason to safeguard them." A muffled growl at his feet made him look down. His jaw dropped. "Emily, I don't want to alarm you, but there's an enormous dog on the hearth."

Emily laughed out loud. "Father, don't be silly. This is Keeper. He found me on the moors today."

The reverend took in every detail about Keeper, from the enormous length of him to his pointed white teeth, dripping with saliva. Emily waited patiently, knowing her father would give in.

"Has Charlotte seen him yet?" he asked in a resigned voice.

"She's already been introduced," Emily assured him. "She adores Keeper."

He raised his eyebrows. "I rather doubt that." He glanced about the small room as though Charlotte was concealed somewhere. "Where is she?"

Even accompanied by Branwell, Emily knew her father would worry about Charlotte out so late. Lying effortlessly, she said, "I think she's in bed. She was very tired."

"She needs her rest," Rev. Brontë said. "She takes so much upon herself."

"And she doesn't let us forget it," Emily said.

"That's unkind, Emily."

"I know. I'll be better." Emily glanced down at her story. Perhaps her father could help her fill in the gaps in Harry's history. "Father, do you recall everyone you've ever buried?"

Rev. Brontë was used to Emily's rapid changes of subject. "There are so many, but I try to give each one a proper farewell. I'd probably remember."

Suddenly she realized she had neglected to ask Harry his mother's name. Charlotte would never have made such an error. With a flash of inspiration, she said, "What about old Mr. Heaton's daughter?"

He shot Emily a surprised glance. "That poor girl."

"In what way?" Emily asked with an avidity that startled her father. Usually she was supremely uninterested in the parish happenings.

"Rachel Heaton was the apple of her father's eye. He was planning a fine marriage for her, to another mill owner."

"But she had other ideas?" Emily asked.

"She spent a few months in Bradford with family and she formed a liaison with a very unsuitable character. Rachel was with child before the Heaton family could do anything about it. They married her off to the fellow—Casson, his name was. My old friend Rev. Smythe officiated. I remember him mentioning he had never seen a sadder bride."

"What happened to her?"

"Things went from bad to worse. Casson was a drunk and he beat her badly. He died soon thereafter, and Rachel came home to have her baby. Her father didn't want to take her back, but I prevailed upon him to do the decent thing."

Could Harry's story be any more tragic, Emily wondered. "How did Casson die?"

"He burned to death in a fire caused by his own drunken carelessness," her father said.

"How horrible!" Emily said, but her mind was conjuring up delightfully gruesome images of the scene. What an ending to a chapter. How could the reader not turn the page?

"You can never be too cautious about fire," her father said sternly. He walked to the fireplace and checked the bucket of water was full. It was an unbreakable rule of the household that a bucket be stationed near every fireplace. "You can never be too careful."

Emily's eyes went to the bare windows and carpetless stone floor. Her father's obsession with fire kept the house inhospitable in summer and freezing in winter.

"It was a merciful deliverance for Rachel," Rev. Brontë continued. "But the Heatons never forgave her for marrying beneath them, nor the boy for the sin of being born."

"So Harry ran away?"

"How do you know his name?" Rev. Brontë asked, his attention sharpened.

Emily thought quickly and responded with a half-truth. "I remember him from when we used to go to the library at Ponden Hall."

"Oh, yes." He twisted his long fingers together. "You see, I'm rather at odds with Robert Heaton. Why this sudden interest in his family?"

"Just curiosity," Emily said. "I wondered if Rachel was still alive."

"I don't recall burying her." He closed his eyes and put his hands together as though he were praying. It was a familiar mannerism to his daughter as he dredged his prodigious memory. "No, definitely not. But I also haven't seen her in quite a long time. She wasn't at her father's funeral."

"That's very strange, isn't it?"

"Perhaps she moved away. It's none of our affair." He kissed Emily on the top of her head. "Good night, my dear. Don't stay up too late. It's already ten o'clock."

Emily heard his heavy footsteps climbing the stairs, pausing to wind his clock. Her father's routine was a reassuring sameness every evening, as sure as the sun rising or the winds blowing across the moor. And his memory was to be relied upon: Rachel Heaton was probably still alive. Harry would be relieved. She returned to her story, confident she had a satisfactory ending.

She was filling up her last page of clean paper when she heard the front door open. Emily recognized Branwell's tread by the thumping his boots made on the back stairs. A moment later he came tramping down again. He avoided the dining room altogether and, to her surprise, she heard him going into their father's study.

She rose quickly and moved soundlessly to the study. She threw open the door and said, "Branwell!"

He was standing at her father's bookcase, his hand on one of the parish registers. He leapt backwards. "Emily, you startled me!"

"What are you doing in here?" she asked, watching his face carefully. Branwell had always been a terrible liar; his lip twitched whenever he uttered a falsehood.

"Just straightening up Father's office," he said, his bottom lip flapping like a fish's on a hook.

The office was as neat as a new pin. Her arms crossed, Emily waited for a better explanation.

"I don't have to explain myself to you, Emily. Remember I'm the elder!" He pushed past her. Emily sniffed the air in the office. She smelt a sweetness, like incense. But not the holy kind used by the Catholics. This was a muskier, more masculine smell hanging oddly about Branwell's person.

She caught him in the hall where he was putting on his coat. Mindful of her father sleeping upstairs, Emily whispered, "Where is Charlotte? I thought she was with you!"

Branwell's handsome face distorted with a sneer. "Charlotte? Why would I know where she is? She's even worse than you when it comes to nursemaiding me." With a bang of the front door, he was gone.

She tried to go back to her work, but her words had deserted her. Where was Charlotte? Emily might stay out all night in the rain, but Charlotte never would. In fact, Charlotte had never missed supper before. She might be hurt or lost. Emily considered going to her father, but rejected the idea out of hand. The last thing she wanted was her father wondering what mischief his daughters got into after sunset.

She had seen Charlotte last in the afternoon when she had stormed out muttering about Branwell. But he had denied knowing anything. Briefly Emily considered the trustworthiness of her brother. She shook her head—she could not rely on anything he said. She'd find him and make him help her find their sister before their father realized anything was amiss. She'd start with the Black Bull, the nearest pub.

Emily considered bringing Keeper but reluctantly decided to leave him behind. Fondling his ears, she whispered, "Keeper, I don't know you well enough yet. You might do anything." Keeper whimpered, but settled back down on the floor.

She slipped on her thick leather walking shoes and let herself out the kitchen door. The rain had stopped. The cherry tree in the front garden dripped and the cobblestones glistened. She kept to the shadows of the buildings along the steep street until it leveled out in front of the pub. A drunkard propped himself against the building as though he was needed to hold it up. Stepping over him, she pressed her face to the dirty window and peered inside.

There was her brother, a fiery bantam rooster crowing at the bar. He had a row of empty glasses in front of him. Branwell didn't have any money—how was he managing to get drunk every night? She stilled the impulse to rush inside and confront him. Even Emily didn't dare to risk her reputation—or, worse, to embarrass her father—by going inside the pub late at night.

Rubbing a patch of grime from the window, Emily watched Branwell lift his glass and speak for a full minute. Judging from the laughter of the men around the bar, Branwell was waxing eloquent. When he wanted to be, her brother was excellent company. He toasted a tall bearded fellow standing beside him who looked vaguely familiar—but then so did all the men in the bar. Emily went to church each week to please her father, but she didn't pay a whit of attention to his parishioners.

The bearded man was dark and well dressed. He pulled out a pound note and slapped it on the bar and the bartender began pouring drinks for the crowd.

Emily watched for the better part of an hour. No one came out of the pub, not while someone else was paying for the drinks. At least she now knew how her penniless brother afforded his debauchery. Emily fumed, knowing she might wait all night for them to finish and she'd be no closer to finding Charlotte. The more hours that passed, the greater the likelihood Charlotte was in trouble.

Finally Branwell half-slid off his stool. Laughing, he righted himself. The bearded man took his arm and led him toward the door. Emily was surprised her hot-tempered brother didn't protest. She had just enough time to duck around the corner before the pub door slammed open. She was still close enough to overhear their conversation.

Supporting Branwell with a strong arm around his waist, the bearded man said urgently, "You'll remember what I said? It must be done immediately." His pale blue eyes reflected the lamplight.

Slurring his words, Branwell assured him, "Of course. I tried tonight but I was prevented by my sister."

"Your sister worries me. She's too curious for my tastes."

"I can take care of her," Branwell muttered.

"Remember, if you don't keep her out of my way, I'll take matters into my own hands."

"Don't worry, Brother," Branwell said. Emily couldn't help but wonder if Branwell and his "Brother" were speaking at cross-purposes.

Emily searched her memory, but she couldn't recall having met the bearded man. He must be speaking of Charlotte. What on earth did Charlotte have to do with all of this?

"Don't call me Brother," growled the man. "You know the penalty." He drew his finger across his throat and Branwell stumbled back fearfully. Emily, in the shadows, narrowed her eyes. Who was this man and why was he threatening her family?

For the next few minutes, Emily trailed behind as the bearded man helped Branwell up the steep hill. Branwell was deposited at the parsonage but Emily continued to follow the stranger, hoping he would lead her to Charlotte. Emily kept a safe distance behind him, glad there was enough moon to light the way.

When he emerged onto the moors, Emily left him to the path while she walked just parallel to him in the brush. It was tougher going, but there was less chance of him seeing her. Not that he was likely to notice anyone; he was stumbling as though he, too, had overindulged in drink.

The bearded man headed west, Emily not far behind. When the man took the turn leading to Ponden Hall, the

Heaton manor, Emily began to suspect she knew his name after all. She realized he had the same cornflower-blue eyes as Harry. This must be Robert Heaton, Harry's cruel uncle.

After much huffing, he reached the summit of the long hill overshadowing Ponden Hall. Emily waited at the crest of the hill and watched as he stumbled down the track and into the comfort of the substantial fieldstone house.

After Robert went inside, she saw a light appear on the second floor. She remembered this was the library. She could see him quite clearly, pouring himself another glass of whiskey, then sitting at a desk and looking at some papers.

She sat on the peat, her knees drawn up to her chest, watching him. Was this a wild goose chase? She had no proof this man knew anything about Charlotte, only that Charlotte had irritated him. It was no crime to be aggravated by Charlotte—it was the constant condition of anyone who knew her!

Did she dare just knock on the door and ask if he knew where Charlotte was? But this was the man Harry had described as dangerous. Emily clenched her fist and pounded her leg in frustration. She didn't know what to do.

Suddenly a steely grip immobilized her shoulder. Emily started to scream. A rough hand covered her mouth.

I lost consciousness: for the second time
in my life—only the second time—
I became insensible from terror.

CHAPTER SIXTEEN

The sound of footsteps and voices faded away. The Masons did not know Charlotte had overheard their most secret rites and rituals. For the moment she was safe. She pushed against the lid of the box. It wouldn't budge. She shoved again. The darkness and the silence pressed on her, squeezing her breath from her body. Charlotte began panting, the noise of her breathing filling the small space. You're behaving like a trapped animal, she told herself. Stay calm. Keep your wits about you.

But fear, raw and bleak as a February storm, threatened to overwhelm her. What would her family think when she didn't come home? They might never know what became of her. Would Branwell finally realize what a wonderful sister he had lost? Emily would finally be sorry she had been so hateful. Tabby would weep whenever she peeled her potatoes, remembering Miss Charlotte and her funny bossy ways. Father . . . he would mourn his little Charlotte.

A scream erupted from her and reverberated off the walls of the chest. She pounded the lid with her fists, kicked with her boots. Pressing her body from one side to the other, she tried to rock the chest, but it was too heavy.

"Help me!" she shouted. "Branwell! John Brown! Anyone! Please help me!"

It was no use. The silence grew more oppressive. The heat was unbearable. If her body was ever found, her father would not even need to spend money on a coffin—they could use the chest. It would sit on the altar in their church, and then John Brown would open the family plot and shove Charlotte inside. At least she would be reunited with Maria and Elizabeth. With a forlorn whimper, Charlotte thought for the first time Emily would envy her sister.

How ironic was it that she had often callously placed her Angrian heroines in situations exactly similar to this one? But those women had heroes to rescue them. Charlotte had no one. She would die shrouded in velvet. Alone. She would never know true love. Never marry. Never have children of her own. Never write a great novel. Her future snuffed out like a candle.

Was it her imagination or was the air getting thicker and closer? Her head swam and each breath rasped her throat. Charlotte felt herself slipping . . . slipping . . . slipping into oblivion.

They forgot everything the minute they were
together again: at least the minute they had
contrived some naughty plan of revenge;
and many a time I've cried to myself to
watch them growing more reckless daily . . .

CHAPTER SEVENTEEN

*E*mily clawed at the fingers pressing into her lips, smothering her scream. There was a whisper in her ear, but the blood rushing to her head drowned out the muffled words. With her other hand, she reached around on the ground, feeling for anything to use as a weapon. Grabbing a loose rock, she smashed at her attacker's hand.

"Ow, Emily! That hurt!" She recognized the aggrieved whisper.

"Harry?" she asked, dropping the rock.

"Why did you do that?" he asked.

"You attacked me!" Emily struggled to get her breath back. "Did you think I wouldn't defend myself?"

"I didn't want you to cry out," he said. Sullenly he added, "But I didn't expect you to fight like a tiger." Harry dropped to the ground next to her. "I should have known better."

Emily smiled to herself. "What are you doing here?"

"I heard someone moving about. More to the point, why are you here?"

Emily said, "I was following your uncle." She pointed at Ponden Hall, where Robert Heaton's silhouette could still be seen at the library window. "My sister is missing. And he knows something, I'm sure of it."

"How long has your sister been gone?" Harry's concern felt like a warm blanket wrapped around Emily's shoulders.

"Since this afternoon. It's not like her." Emily bit her lip. She explained how Charlotte had left the house on a mysterious errand connected with Branwell and had never returned. Branwell had claimed not to know where Charlotte was, but Emily didn't believe him.

She recounted following Branwell to the pub where she'd seen Robert buying drinks for him. "At first I didn't know who he was. But he called Branwell 'Brother.'"

"Ah." Harry's eyes brightened in the new moon. "And today is Friday."

"What happens on Friday?"

"It's lodge night. Robert's a Freemason, didn't you know?"

Emily shook her head, her mind racing as she tried to connect Charlotte's disappearance with the secretive Masons. "I don't know anything about the Masons."

"Nor do they want you to." Harry went on, "My grandfather was a Mason and he had Robert join as soon as he turned twenty-one. Every Friday they went to Newall Street for the lodge meeting. I used to follow him there. If he called Branwell 'Brother,' then your brother's a Freemason, too."

Emily got to her feet and began to pace around on the narrow ledge. "Branwell can't be a Mason. We would know."

"Does he have friends you don't know about? Maybe he makes odd gestures with his hands when he's talking to men in town?"

Emily nodded slowly, realizing just how odd Branwell's behavior had been lately. "And somehow he has plenty of money for drinking."

"It sounds as if Branwell has just been initiated into the lodge. Robert must have been his sponsor—that's why he was buying the drinks."

"You said Robert joined at twenty-one. Branwell is only eighteen."

"Sometimes they make exceptions."

Emily frowned. "But there's nothing special about Branwell. He's neither wealthy nor important."

"I remember him a little bit from when we were younger." Harry stroked his chin thoughtfully. "He was always good company, and I envied his breadth of reading."

"Breadth but no depth," Emily sighed. "Branwell is all promise and no accomplishments."

"They must have a use for him." He glanced down at Ponden Hall. Emily's eyes followed. As they watched, Robert turned down the lamp in the library and the windows went dark. "But what does this have to do with your sister?"

"Your uncle ordered Branwell to make her mind her own business."

"Perhaps Charlotte knows something dangerous to the Masons," Harry suggested.

"The Masons grossly overestimate Branwell's ability to influence my sister." Emily tapped her fist against her lips. "If Charlotte thinks she's in the right, it would be easier to turn back floodwaters than to divert her from her purpose."

"And you say she mentioned Newall Street?"

Emily looked up and met Harry's eyes. "What if she tried to stop Branwell from joining the Masons? What if she made trouble at a meeting?"

"The Masons claim they are a fraternity dedicated to charitable works—but it's not coincidental they are all powerful men. They value their privacy and threaten death to anyone who penetrates their secrets."

"Would they harm a woman?" Emily asked, fearing the answer.

"The Freemasons are mostly decent men," Harry said slowly. "I'm sure they wouldn't hurt Charlotte."

"Then why hasn't she come back?" Emily asked. She took a deep breath and steeled her resolve. "I'm going to that lodge."

"Wait! It's too dangerous," Harry said.

"If Charlotte is being held there, all the more reason for me to hurry." Emily started to run down the hill.

She heard thudding footsteps behind her and she slowed as the land flattened out. "Why are you following me?"

"It's too risky to go alone," Harry said, panting a little.

"To protect my family—I'll risk anything," Emily declared, her voice ringing in the darkness. Then more gently, "You should understand. What wouldn't you do to save your mother?"

"I'll go with you, then."

"I'd welcome that, but you can't come into town," Emily pointed out. "You said it yourself; your only advantage is secrecy."

"Then I lose my advantage." Harry squared his shoulders. "I cannot permit you to do this alone."

Emily reached out and touched his hand. "Harry," she said gently. "You do realize you couldn't stop me?"

He grasped her hand in his and brought it to his lips. "If I can't stop you, then I must help you."

Emily paused, her whole world narrowed to the soft pressure of his lips on her hand. They were alone in the dark and Harry was kissing her hand. A scene from one of her stories. Or, more likely, Charlotte's. But this heroine had more important things to do. She snatched back her hand.

"Let's go, then. Charlotte may be imprisoned or hurt or . . ." Emily's lurid imagination provided altogether too many awful fates that might have befallen her sister.

"I have to get a few things," he said, turning toward his camp.

Emily waited impatiently. A few minutes later, he returned carrying a shielded lantern. Emily's keen eyes noticed his pistol was stuck in his waistband.

As they made their way back to town, Emily broke the silence. "I asked my father about your mother. He conducts every funeral in Haworth, but he doesn't remember burying your mother."

"Is he sure?"

"Well, to be certain, we'd have to ask him to consult the parish records. My father doesn't allow anyone but himself to touch them. But your family is important enough that I think we can rely on his memory."

"That's a great relief," Harry said. They continued hurrying along the path. After a moment he continued, "After we find your sister, may I ask you for a favor?"

"Anything," Emily said with sincerity. "But first we must find Charlotte."

The clouds rolled back in to cover the moon and obscure their vision. As they walked down the path past the parsonage, scattered drops of rain were making the stones slick and slippery. The town was dark and even the Black Bull was shuttered and quiet.

Harry led her down a narrow alley to the tall house at the end. "This is it." Swinging the lantern so it illuminated the cornerstone of the house, he pointed out the symbols of Freemasonry: the chisel and builder's square.

"It's a substantial house," Emily said thoughtfully. "I somehow thought their meetings would be held in a lonely barn or a damp cave."

"The Freemasons have money and all the property they need," Harry said with a tinge of bitterness.

"How do we get in?" Emily asked. The front door looked unassailable, and visible to any passersby on Main Street besides. They went around to the side entrance and found the door loose on its hinges. Harry forced open the door with his shoulder. The house stayed completely silent. Holding the lantern high, Harry said, "Let me go first."

"I think not," Emily retorted, taking the lamp. "Charlotte is my sister." She led the way up the stairs to a spacious antechamber with a large ornate door. She pushed the door and it opened with a loud creak that made them both jump.

"This must be where they meet," Harry said in a hushed tone.

Emily took the lantern and shone its light on the walls. "Branwell painted this one," she said, pointing to a portrait. "It's our sexton, John Brown." She turned back to Harry. "Is *everyone* a Mason?" She ticked off on her fingers. "My brother, your uncle, Mr. Brown. But where is Charlotte?"

Her voice rose on the final words. Harry held up a hand. "Listen!"

Emily fell silent. There was a faint moaning sound from a decorative chest in the corner of the room. Holding fiercely to hope, Emily crossed the room to the chest. She slid the latch open and lifted the lid.

"Charlotte!" she cried.

Her sister, pale and wan, blinked at the lantern light. "Emily, is that you?"

"Yes, Charlotte. I'm here!" Emily said.

Harry gathered Charlotte up in his arms. She looked into his face and murmured, "My duke!" Then she fainted dead away.

The next thing I remember is, waking up with a
feeling as if I had had a frightful nightmare,
and seeing before me a terrible red glare,
crossed with thick black bars. . . .
In five minutes more the cloud of bewilderment
dissolved: I knew quite well
that I was in my own bed, and that
the red glare was the nursery fire.

CHAPTER EIGHTEEN

*C*harlotte woke in a cold sweat, her chest heaving and her
fingers clawing at her blankets. Trapped in a velvet coffin, she
had suffocated. Or had she? She opened her eyes and found
herself in her narrow bed in the tiny room she shared with
Emily. She inhaled and tasted fresh air off the moors, full of
rain. Never before had her tongue fully appreciated the tang of
wind and freedom.

"Emily—how many times have I told you to close the window?" she mumbled, but her heart wasn't in it. There was no answer. "Emily?" Charlotte propped herself up to see her sister's bed. It was empty, the bedclothes flung about every which way.

Suddenly it all came rushing back. Charlotte had been rescued from that chest by Emily. And a handsome young man. She dimly remembered him gathering her in his strong arms, like a scene from Angria come to life!

Did it really happen? Or had she finally lost the ability to distinguish between her fictional world and real life? The thought terrified her. She clasped her hands together and prayed for clarity.

As if to answer her, the church bell began tolling. It was the first call for the congregation to come to worship. Charlotte bolted upright. Her father would never forgive her if she missed his sermon. Why hadn't Emily or Tabby wakened her? She threw back the covers, noticing for the first time she was wearing her night shift.

Reaching for her dress from the day before, she stopped and stared at her once-immaculate dress. It was covered with dust and bits of red velvet. One of the narrow sleeves was torn at the shoulder seam, and her careful embroidery on the collar was stained with perspiration. She brought the fabric to her nose and recoiled from the unmistakable scent of fear. Her hand brushed against her cheek and she winced. Her knuckles were cut and bruised from pounding on the chest lid.

Her adventure had really happened. She sighed with relief; she was not insane.

If she was not mad, then her brother and sister owed her some explanations. Since Emily was gone, she would start with Branwell. She pulled on another dress and hurried to his room. She knocked but there was no answer.

She pushed open the door. His room was one of the largest in the house, but its only window looked out on the privy. A chisel and a builder's square lay on his battered desk, additional proof that the events of the night before had not been a dream.

Branwell had tossed his coat on the back of a chair. Hesitating only for a moment, Charlotte decided her need for answers outweighed Branwell's privacy. She checked his pockets and found a piece of paper. It was covered with her father's fine script; the same word was repeated over and over.

The church bells rang again, more insistently this time. She rushed downstairs and out through the garden to the churchyard. It was raining. The way the mud sucked at her shoes made her realize it had rained every day since she returned home. Where did all the water go? She gave herself a little shake; such whimsical considerations were Emily's domain, not hers.

As she made her way past the crowded graveyard, she was relieved to see other latecomers from town and the moors beyond, drawn by the urgent chiming of the bells.

The church was full, as it always was on Sunday. The parish of Haworth was a large one and there were many devout worshippers: rich, poor, the educated, and those whose wits were dulled by constant backbreaking labor.

Once inside, she kept a decorous pace as she walked to the family pew. She passed the Heaton pew, the short-tempered Robert Heaton its only occupant. He glimpsed her out of the corner of his eye and turned to watch her as she passed. Charlotte kept facing forward. What would he do if he knew what she had witnessed the day before? She flexed her sore hands. What was a little pain to scoring such a victory over Heaton's smugness and arrogance?

The Brontë pew was an enclosed box in the front of the church to the left of the altar, squeezed in under the organ loft. The pew walls were higher than her waist, and the family name was painted on the low door. She slipped inside and found Branwell and Emily clad in their Sunday best, only slightly damp from the weather.

Charlotte sat next to Branwell. His eyes were bloodshot and he winced with every toll of the bell. He glanced at Charlotte, but said nothing. Emily sat in the corner, wearing a bored expression. She came to church only because their father insisted. When Emily saw her sister, she smiled, the first true welcome Charlotte had received from her.

The bells stopped their ringing and the organ began to play, causing their wooden pew to vibrate in tune. Emily took malicious pleasure in the pained expression on her brother's drink-addled face. Out of the corner of her eye she saw the barrel shape of John Brown patrolling the aisle. It was his job to knob sleeping parishioners with his stick. His mighty arms had been strengthened by years of working stone; he seldom had to poke twice.

From their front-row pew, the Brontë siblings had an excellent view of Rev. Brontë as he mounted the narrow stairs leading to his pulpit high above the congregation. He wore a white surplice that suited his tall frame. He carried no notes; he never did, and he could quote excruciatingly long biblical passages from memory. But his sermons were rousing as well as scholarly. Lately, he had addressed the inequities between the rich and poor. But the reverend's position depended on the support of those rich mill own-ers. Charlotte might fear he would not be circumspect, but Emily hoped he would lay into the mill owners with the ver-bal equivalent of a scourge.

Rev. Brontë raised his hand to gather the congregation's attention. His normal mild manner deserted him in the pulpit. When he opened his mouth, his voice was authority itself. The voice of God on earth.

"Let me quote this passage from the book of Ezekiel."

Charlotte sighed; Ezekiel did not bode well for a tactful sermon.

"'The people of the land have practiced oppression and committed robbery, and they have wronged the poor and needy. . . . Thus I have poured out My indignation on them; I have consumed them with the fire of My wrath,' declares the Lord God," Rev. Brontë thundered.

Then in a calmer voice he said, "Let us reflect for a moment about what these words mean to us here in Haworth. The mill owners are bringing in new machines that eliminate jobs. They are depriving workers of a decent wage. Children are starving and families are being ripped asunder by the poorhouses. Can the owners claim they have *not* wronged the poor?"

There was a stirring in the congregation. Emily settled in to enjoy her father's tirade.

Charlotte looked round to watch the mill owners, particularly Robert Heaton. His brows were drawn together in a fierce scowl, and she could see his hands were white from gripping the pew railing. The paleness made a recent scar on the top of his hand all the more visible. As she watched, he made an odd gesture with his thumb and forefinger to another rich mill owner. That man signaled another in the same way. Secret messages were flying furiously about the church.

Charlotte felt a deep foreboding. This meant trouble for her father, she was sure of it. Rather than exhaust herself with worry, she leaned back in the pew and closed her eyes, reducing her father's ringing tones to a quiet refrain behind her thoughts. She wanted to remember each terrible detail of last night's adventure. Now that she had known real terror, she wondered whether the melodrama she wrote into her scenes from Angria was convincing. Perhaps she couldn't express any true emotion until she had felt it herself? Charlotte felt as though she were on the brink of a great revelation that might change her writing forever.

The sermon ended exactly one hour after it had begun. It was never a minute overlong, even though the reverend never consulted his watch. After some parish business, the congregation was dismissed.

Without discussing the matter, Charlotte, Emily, and Branwell waited until their father emerged from the vestry. He was met by Robert Heaton leading a group of mill owners. Heaton's jaw, with his pointed black beard, was the sharp edge of a wedge of discontented parishioners. Branwell hung back, looking ill as he watched his Freemason sponsor accost his father. Charlotte tried to pass him to stand by her father's side, but Branwell blocked her way.

"You always interfere, Charlotte, but not this time," he said, his eyes fixed on Heaton.

"That's Robert Heaton, isn't it?" Emily whispered to Charlotte. Charlotte gave her a sharp glance, but nodded. "I've never seen him up close." Emily rested her elbows on the pew door and watched, curious to see Harry's uncle in action.

"Brontë!" Heaton said.

"Mr. Heaton. Gentlemen," Rev. Brontë greeted the delegation. His voice was gentle and meek again, as though the mantle of justice weighed on his shoulders only when he preached. "Do you *all* wish to speak with me?"

"I've warned you before: Stop preaching we are monsters," Heaton growled. There was a murmur of agreement among the other men. "We own the means of production and we are entitled to make a profit. The more successful we are, the better it is for our workers."

"With all due respect, Mr. Heaton," Rev. Brontë began crossly, "that is not true. You grow richer but the workers suffer for it. For instance, I know for a fact that just one of your new looms deprives two men of gainful employment. What will happen to their families?"

Heaton glanced around at his fellow owners and said, "Brontë, it's no business of yours how we run our mills. And you're just encouraging the malcontents." The others were nodding.

Emily's attention sharpened. Last night, after delivering Charlotte to the parsonage, Harry had asked Emily to help him gain access to Ponden Hall.

It would be dangerous, Emily knew, but her gratitude outweighed her caution. And if she were not mistaken, an opportunity to repay her debt had presented itself. She pushed open the pew door and before Branwell could try and stop her, she strode over to the group of angry men.

Heaton was still talking. "We pay the bulk of the fees to maintain this church and your position here. You have forced our hand. Stop preaching your incitements to riot, or we'll be speaking to your bishop about your future in Haworth."

Rev. Brontë took a breath to defend his views, but Emily interrupted him.

"Father, excuse me for interrupting." Although she spoke to her father, she watched Heaton closely.

Branwell frowned. "What is she doing?" he asked Charlotte. "The two of you don't know how to mind your own business."

Charlotte wondered the same thing. What could Emily want with Mr. Heaton? Perhaps she was going to confront him for luring Branwell into the Masons. But how could she know?

Rev. Brontë was dismayed. "Emily, my dear, go to the parsonage. I'm in the middle of an important conversation."

"I will, Father, but first I wanted to introduce myself to Mr. Heaton." She held out her hand to him. "I am Emily Brontë."

Robert Heaton was taken aback, but after a moment he took her hand.

"Mr. Heaton, you may not recall," Emily said, "but when I was younger, I used to visit your library."

"Emily, this is not the time!" Rev. Brontë whispered.

Visibly discomfited, Heaton nevertheless answered civilly. "My father was very proud of his books. Perhaps we can discuss it after my conversation is finished?"

"I won't be a moment. I wondered if you would mind if I borrowed a volume or two?" Emily asked sweetly.

There was a quiet chuckle from one of the other owners. Charlotte saw Heaton could not refuse Emily's request without looking churlish. "Well . . . I don't see why not."

"May I come today? I've nothing to read, and I'm at my wits' end."

"Of course." Heaton was impatient for her to go. "Just tell my housekeeper I said to admit you."

"Thank you." Having achieved what she wanted, Emily was about to slip away when she noticed a nasty cut on Heaton's right hand. In a flash she realized she could make a very good guess as to the identity of the parsonage's intruder. "That's a vicious cut. I hope you haven't injured yourself too badly, Mr. Heaton." Before he could respond, she slipped away and disappeared in the milling crowd.

Heaton was momentarily speechless and Rev. Brontë seized the moment. "Gentlemen, if you would like to continue this conversation, perhaps you might call on me in the parsonage, where such business should be conducted. I shall be available after two o'clock." He walked away, leaving the owners thwarted and confused.

"Father should be more deferential," Branwell said to Charlotte. "Robert Heaton is too important a man to offend."

"Where are your loyalties?" Charlotte tackled her brother. "Your fine friend Mr. Heaton wants to destroy our father."

"I don't know what you are talking about," Branwell said with a sullen glare.

"Stop acting the fool," Charlotte snapped. "He's using you." That was as far as she dared go without revealing what she knew about Branwell and his new friends.

"Charlotte, you are talking nonsense," Branwell protested. Then, with an air of inspiration, he added, "Heaton's like a brother to me. A refreshing change to be accepted among men, not trapped in a henhouse with my sisters." As Heaton left the church, Branwell's gaze followed him with near adoration.

Charlotte shook her head. "If you aren't careful, you'll bring ruin upon the whole family." Without another word, she hurried out of the church, heedless of the drizzle. Heaton was halfway down the hill on his way into town. She followed, struggling to keep her footing on the slippery stones.

"Mr. Heaton," she called. "A word, if you please."

He looked behind him and shook his head irritably. "Another Brontë? What have I done to deserve such attention from your family?"

Charlotte stopped above him on the hill. It gave her the illusion of being able to meet his eyes at an equal height. "What do you want with Branwell?" she asked directly.

"I beg your pardon?"

"I know you've inveigled Branwell into some scheme." The Freemasons' threats still rang in Charlotte's ears, so she kept her questions circumspect.

Heaton's eyes bored into hers. "What has he told you?"

"Nothing!" Charlotte said. "But I'm very observant and I can't help wondering if your scheme has anything to do with your sister Rachel."

Heaton's face turned red and he spat out his words. "I've warned you before to stay out of my business. I won't be thwarted or questioned by a woman." He turned away and continued to walk rapidly down the hill.

Charlotte exhaled and put her hand on a wall to keep her equilibrium. "He won't be thwarted by a woman, will he?" she thought. "Let's see if Robert Heaton can be undone by *two* Brontë sisters."

"No books!" I exclaimed. "How do you contrive to
live here without them? if I may take the liberty to
inquire. Though provided with a large library,
I'm frequently very dull at the Grange; take my
books away, and I should be desperate!"

CHAPTER NINETEEN

*H*eedless of the inclement weather, Emily headed for
the moors. She was wearing her Sunday best, but she couldn't
be bothered to change—every dress was alike to her. Stopping
at home only to collect a shawl to keep off the rain and to bring
Keeper along, she was soon approaching Harry's campsite.
Inside his tent, he was reclining on the cot, reading Byron. He
wore a white linen shirt and his hair was mussed. Emily committed the details of his appearance to memory. For a story
someday, she told herself.

"Don't you think it's time for a new book?" Emily teased.

"Emily!" He leapt to his feet to greet her, smoothing his hair. "What do you mean?"

"Why don't we go to Ponden House?" Emily said.

He was taken aback. "Now?"

"I asked your uncle for permission."

"And he agreed?" Harry was incredulous.

"He didn't have much of a choice." Emily smiled at the memory. "He was with a group of men whose opinion mattered to him. It would have been rude of him to refuse." She looked around the campsite and found the old rope Harry had used to tie up Keeper. "Come here, Keeper."

"His name is Roland." Harry snapped his fingers for the dog to come to him, but Keeper stayed at Emily's side.

"Not anymore." Emily smiled as she tied the rope around Keeper's neck. "If you had thought of him less as property and more like a friend, he might have chosen to stay with you."

"But yet you call him Keeper?" he asked, his dark eyebrows raised questioningly over his laughing blue eyes.

"It's a term of affection," she assured him with a smile.

Keeper whimpered, but Emily spoke firmly. "Now lie down and be quiet." She turned to Harry. "What do you want me to do?"

Harry ran his thumb along his chin. "We have to get into the library. My uncle keeps all his papers there."

"Tell me what to look for," Emily said. "It's too dangerous for you to go; the servants would recognize you in an
instant."

"I can't tell you what to look for—I have to see for myself."
Emily started to speak, but Harry interrupted. "You can let me
in secretly."

Emily raised her eyebrows. "How?"

"Follow me." He led the way up through the light rain to
the rise of ground above the hollow where Ponden Hall was
situated. The great house's stone walls were gloomy and the
porch was covered with moss. There was a stand of malevolent
fir trees, one of which stretched a branch toward the library
window on the second floor, as though it were a ghoul tapping
on the window.

With a mischievous glint in his eye, Harry asked, "Do
you see the door behind the trees there?" He pointed to a spot
below the library windows.

Emily could just make it out.

"It leads to a root cellar. But when I was a boy I discovered
a passage between the cellar and the library. No one seemed to
know about it but me. I hope that's still true."

"A secret passage?" Emily clapped her hands in glee. "But if
there's a way in, why do you need me?"

"The door from the cellar is unlocked, but the library door
is locked. You can only open it from inside the library."

"I wonder why?"

"I think my great-grandfather might have had his troubles with the Crown. This was an escape route to be used in great need. I only found it by accident."

Emily was lost in the past. "When we were children," she said slowly, "I recall you used to disappear mysteriously."

He grinned wickedly. "You couldn't expect me to tell my secret to a mere girl, could you?"

Emily found the idea of a secret passage irresistible, but a vestige of caution, no doubt nurtured by Charlotte, gave her pause. "If you are found in the library," she said very deliberately, "I'm compromised, too. And my father with me."

Harry rocked back on his heels. "You're right. I shouldn't ask for your help, but there is so much at stake." He flushed, and Emily caught her breath at how handsome he looked. "But you are right—what would people say if you broke into Ponden Hall with me? Say the word. I'll find another way."

Emily suddenly grinned, restored to her usual equanimity. "I don't much care what other people think. I never have." A crooked smile on her face, she added, "And we won't be caught."

◼◆◼

Emily took a series of calming breaths before she lifted the knocker. For once, she couldn't control the direction of a story with the stroke of a pen. As she waited for someone to answer the door, she could hear Keeper howling in the distance. With the leaden clouds above, his muffled howls had an ethereal quality. "No wonder Tabby thinks a *gytrash* haunts the moor!" Emily murmured to herself.

Finally the door was opened by a housekeeper. She stared at Emily as though she was trying to place her face. "Yes?"

"It's Grace, isn't it?" Emily found the woman's name lodged deep in her memory. "My name is Emily Brontë."

"The parson's daughter?" Grace asked. "If you're here to see the master, he's not here."

"I just saw Mr. Heaton at church," Emily replied. "He said I could visit the library."

"Did he?" Grace asked suspiciously. "That doesn't sound like him."

"Of course, you could refuse me entry and explain to Mr. Heaton why you turned away his invited guest," Emily said.

The door opened a little wider. "I'm not refusing, miss. I'm just saying the master is particular about who comes into the house."

"Because of his sister?" Emily hazarded. She was rewarded with an indrawn hiss. "Is she here? I'd like to pay my respects."

"She's not here." Grace was shaking her head. "And the less questioning about her the better." Her lips squeezed shut and Emily knew she would get no more information.

"I know the way, Grace. You don't need to take me up." Emily began climbing the stairs, transported for a moment to her childhood. She remembered how the window at the top of the stairs would bathe the landing in light. But today the sun was obscured by black clouds.

It occurred to Emily it had rained at least part of every day for weeks. Perhaps Harry had brought the rain with him. Until the terrible wrong done to him was righted, until his mother was found or avenged, the sun wouldn't return.

The library was exactly the way she remembered it—uncannily so. It was a long paneled room full of bookcases from floor to ceiling. There was a small fire burning—no doubt to keep the damp away from the books. Under glass were the valuable books the children had never been allowed to touch.

There were two comfortable armchairs at the end of the room in front of the fireplace. In the corner, just above the root cellar, Emily guessed, was a bookcase built next to the window jamb. Outside the window the fir tree branches brushed against the panes.

Emily listened at the stairs, but the house was silent. She hurried to the corner bookcase where Harry had told her to look. She removed a stack of old hymnbooks and found a square panel of wood that was slightly different from the rest of the bookcase. She pressed it.

With a loud click, the bookcase swung out. Harry was waiting, covered with cobwebs and dust. "Well done," he said, starting purposefully for the desk in the corner of the room. He began to fan through the papers on it.

"Is there anything useful?" Emily asked.

"Nothing. Uncle Robert is not such a fool," Harry said. "Anything incriminating won't be left in plain sight." He tugged on the drawer of the desk, but it was locked. "Do you see a key anywhere?"

"We don't need a key." For once, Emily's hair was relatively tidy—it was Sunday, after all. Pulling a long pin out of the bun at the back of her head, she knelt at the desk and poked the pin in the lock.

"How on earth do you know how to do that?" Harry asked. "I had no idea a clergyman's daughter could also be a picklock." His face showed his delight in her unexpected skill.

Closing her eyes to better manipulate the lock, Emily said, "I read about it in a novel and I practiced on my brother's desk until I taught myself how to do it."

The lock clicked open.

"You amaze me," Harry said. Heat suffused Emily's face and she was careful not to look at him. He pushed past her and took out the papers from the drawer. Scanning the top document, Harry said, "I don't believe it."

"What is it?" Emily asked, stepping forward, only just restraining herself from snatching the papers out of his hand.

"It's a petition to the magistrate in Leeds to have my mother declared incompetent."

Emily lifted her eyebrows. "Can he do that?"

"He says her mind has been ruined by drink." He turned to Emily, his face pale. "She doesn't drink. Ever. My father was a drunkard—Mother wouldn't touch the stuff."

She placed a hand on his arm. "At least this confirms she's alive," Emily said gently.

His smile was wan. "True. Thank God for that." He returned to the petition. "It's missing a doctor's signature."

"Are there any doctors in the Three Graces Lodge? Wouldn't one Freemason help another?"

He nodded. "There's at least one. Dr. Fitzpatrick. And he's an old friend of my uncle's. Without anyone to speak for my mother, Fitzpatrick would believe whatever Robert told him."

"But why do it at all?" Emily asked. "What does it accomplish?"

Harry paced around the library. "I don't know."

"What is this?" Emily asked, picking up another set of papers in the drawer.

Harry glanced at it. "It's my grandfather's will."

"Did he leave you anything?"

"I doubt it," Harry said. "The old man hated me."

Emily turned up the oil lamp to illuminate the paper. "I leave all my real property, the farms and the mills, to be divided equally between my children, Robert and Rachel Heaton."

"Equally? That doesn't sound like the old curmudgeon. He must have been stricken with an attack of fairness before he died."

Emily read on. "It says, 'If, for any reason, either of my children are legally incapable of managing their affairs, I assign their legal offspring to manage their share of the property. If there are no legitimate heirs, then the remaining sibling will control the entire legacy.'" Emily glanced up from the paper. "What does that mean?"

Harry nodded sagely. "My great-grandfather had a brother who was kicked in the head by a horse. He never woke up, but he didn't die for half a decade. The family feuded over the farms for years. It even went to the courts."

"But you are alive to manage your mother's legacy," Emily pointed out. "What does your uncle gain by declaring her incompetent?"

Harry was distracted as though he were examining and discarding possible explanations. Emily reached past him and took the last item out of the drawer. It was an old leather-bound ledger.

"Harry, this is a registry of marriages from the church in Bradford," Emily cried. "It was stolen last month."

"Why would Robert have this?" Harry asked.

Before Emily could answer, they heard a noise from the stairs. "Quick! Hide!" Emily said. Harry ducked under the desk. Emily moved a chair in front of it and then moved to a bookcase.

Grace shoved open the door, her face avid, no doubt hoping to catch Emily doing something she oughtn't. She was disappointed, as the only thing she saw was Emily lost in contemplation of a rare First Folio of William Shakespeare in the glass cabinet.

"Yes, Grace?" Emily tore her attention from the folio.

Looking abashed, Grace said sullenly, "Would you be wanting tea, miss?"

"Thank you. That would be most welcome." She picked another favorite, a novel of Sir Walter Scott's, and settled in the chair, flipping the pages.

The sound of Grace's footsteps had long faded when there was a whisper from under the desk. "Emily?"

"Oh, Harry!" She jumped up and pulled the chair away so he could emerge. "I'm sorry, I forgot you were there."

He watched her for several seconds as he brushed the dust off his pants. Finally he began to laugh. "Let me guess. You started reading?"

Emily grinned and held up *Ivanhoe*. "Harry, we used to read this same book when we were children. Do you remember?" She held out the book.

Harry opened the cover and stared at the frontispiece. The sternness in his face softened and he began to flip the pages. "I do remember. I remember everything!" Suddenly he threw the book onto the fire.

"Harry!" Emily exclaimed, using the fire tongs to retrieve the book. Fortunately, she thought, she hadn't been examining the Shakespeare.

"I don't want to remember," he said.

Brushing off the precious book, Emily spoke slowly as if Harry were still a child. "No matter what your grandfather and uncle did to you then, there were wonderful stories in your childhood. It would be a great shame to destroy what was good and true because of your family's cruelty."

He glared at her, but she returned his stare until he looked away. "You are right, Emily. After all, *you* were part of my childhood. I don't want to forget that."

"I hear Grace coming back," Emily said. "You must go." He shoved the papers and ledger from the desk into a satchel, ran to the bookcase, and disappeared into the wall. The bookcase was clicking shut just as Grace appeared in the doorway carrying a tray with tea.

"Thank you, Grace," Emily said, taking the tray from the housekeeper.

"You've been in here a long time," Grace said with a sour expression. "Haven't you found something to read yet?"

Emily glanced at the desk and the long room with its floor-to-ceiling bookcase and at the singed book in her hands. "More than I bargained for."

Somebody has plotted something:
you cannot too soon find out who and what it is.

CHAPTER TWENTY

*E*mily ran headlong down the hill that sheltered Harry's campsite hugging the singed edition of *Ivanhoe* to her chest, a trophy of her daring excursion into Heaton territory. The grass was slippery with the mist that had descended on the moor now that the rain had stopped. Arriving out of breath, she found the campsite empty except for Keeper, sprawled by the fire. She exclaimed in disappointment; she wanted to relive her adventure with Harry.

She decided to wait inside the tent. She pulled aside the flap.

"Harry!" He stood in the center of the small room, a shielded candle burning on the trunk. His head was slightly ducked to keep from hitting the ceiling.

"Harry," she said again, then lost her words as her eyes adjusted to the dim light and she took in the sight of him. He wore his trousers and boots and was just shrugging into a clean shirt.

His body was lean and long. He had only a scattering of chest hair. His muscles were marked across his torso as though a Renaissance painter had sketched them in.

"Emily!" His blue eyes widened and he stepped toward her. "I was beginning to worry." His voice dropped to a whisper. "You were so long at Ponden Hall, I was afraid Robert had caught you there."

"I thought I should stay a little longer," Emily said, moving toward him as though drawn by a magnetic force. "To allay any suspicions."

Henry tucked a strand of Emily's damp hair behind her ear. "And did you?" he asked. His fingers lingered, twisted in the lock of hair.

Emily's hand went to her cheek, almost but not quite touching his hand. "Did I what?" she breathed.

"Allay suspicion?" A half step and Harry narrowed the gap between them.

Emily stared at the sheen of moisture on his bare chest. She wondered what it felt like. As though her desire controlled her actions, she placed her palm flat on his chest.

"My brave Emily," he said, his voice husky. "So bold and so lovely."

"No one has ever said that before," Emily said. Suddenly she was in new territory and all her previous habits of indifference and solitude deserted her.

"Then no one has ever seen you like this—fresh from the moors. You are . . . luminous."

She mouthed the word, enjoying the way it pursed her lips. Harry touched her bottom lip with his fingertip, tracing its shape. She leaned in, tilted her head, and pressed her mouth to his for an instant. His lips were soft to the touch and his freshly shaved face was smooth against her skin.

"Emily," he breathed. The single word made her senses swim and she pressed her body against his. His arms surrounded her in his embrace. He smelled of wood smoke and library dust. His mouth came down hard on hers. Emily felt the warmth of his body. She returned his kiss, matching his passion with her own.

"Emily!" As though a butcher's cleaver had crashed between them, a shrill voice drove them apart. Charlotte stood in the opening of the tent, her face pale and shocked.

Breathing hard, Emily wheeled on her sister. "Charlotte, get out!"

Without saying a word, Charlotte grabbed Emily's hand and hauled her outside the tent.

"Charlotte, what are you doing?" Emily shook off Charlotte's hand.

"Arriving just in time, I suspect," Charlotte cried. "Emily, how could you put yourself in such a compromising position? You were alone with a half-dressed man. And you were . . ."

"Kissing him!" Emily interrupted. "It was lovely. I'd like to do it again. So go home and stay out of my business."

Crossing her arms in front of her chest, Charlotte said, "I would be failing Father if I left you unchaperoned."

Emily recognized Charlotte at her most stubborn. "How did you even know I was here?"

"I was watching Ponden Hall. After that scene you made at church, I knew you wouldn't wait long to do whatever it was you wanted to do there. I followed you when you left. And a good thing, too. I arrived before you completely ruined your reputation."

"Spare me your platitudes. You forget I've read all your Angria stories. You would throw yourself into the arms of the duke if only you had the courage." Emily frowned and added, "And if he were real, of course."

"Courage? You think it takes courage to meet a man secretly and misbehave?"

A puzzled expression on her face, Emily repeated, "Misbehave?"

Charlotte nodded violently. "You were kissing him!"

"So?" Emily shrugged.

Charlotte shook her head. "Emily, poor gentlewomen like us—with intelligence but no dowries—we cannot afford to tarnish our reputations. Not if we ever hope to marry."

"Marry? Who wants to get married? Have you seen the women around here? Walking hangdog at their husbands' heels, with bruised eyes and no freedom?" Emily threw out her arms. "I'll never marry anyone!"

"Sssh! He'll hear you!" Charlotte hissed.

"So?"

Her lips pursed and her eyes bulging, Charlotte made a rude sound. "You're impossible!"

Emily started to laugh. "If you could see the expression on your face!"

"Who is he, anyway?" Charlotte asked.

"I was wondering when you would ask. Don't you recognize him?" Emily asked slyly.

"He rescued me last night, didn't he?" Charlotte said, her eyes glassy for a moment as she relived the moment he took her up in his arms.

"You called him your duke," Emily said. "And then you fainted."

Charlotte closed her eyes and blushed. "What must he think of me?"

"Frankly, we were both too busy wondering why you were locked in a chest at the Masonic lodge," Emily said. "Did they kidnap you?"

"The Freemasons didn't even know I was there."

"Truly?" Emily's voice had newfound respect in it.

"Branwell has become one of them. I snuck in to listen to their most secret meeting. I heard many things of interest but at the last minute, purely by mischance, I was locked in the chest."

"That's wonderful," Emily said, her admiration warm and genuine.

"It certainly is." A masculine voice made both girls' heads whip round toward the tent. "I should have known any sister of Emily's would also be as brave as a lion." Harry was fully dressed now, his coat decorously buttoned over his shirt. He was cautious as he stepped outside. "Is it safe for me to come out?"

Charlotte caught her breath. He was as handsome as she recollected from the night before. His dark wavy hair set off his piercing blue eyes. He could be the very model for her duke. What would it be like for him to take her in his arms? She could always ask Emily, Charlotte thought sourly.

Emily gestured for Harry to come closer. "Harry, this is my sister, Charlotte."

Charlotte pursed her lips, unsure of what was proper. She didn't want to come off as a shrew, but she had found them locked in a disreputable embrace.

"Charlotte, don't be a prude," Emily scolded. "Each of us is an adult and entitled to do what we want, so long as no one else is hurt."

Catching her bottom lip between her teeth, Charlotte still hesitated.

Harry stepped forward. "Harry Casson," he said, holding out his hand. Charlotte looked down at it, conscious of her sister's censorious eye upon her. She made up her mind and took his hand in hers. His fingers were long and fine-boned, but she felt the calluses on his palm.

"Charlotte Brontë," she said. "I don't believe we were properly introduced last night."

"A pleasure to meet you."

"I must thank you for coming to my rescue," Charlotte said, feeling the heat creep up her neck and cheeks.

"Think nothing of it," Harry said, a smile on his lips. He glanced between Charlotte and Emily, as if wondering how they could be sisters; one so tall and wild, the other tiny and prim. "How did you come to be spying on the Freemasons?"

"I was trying to protect my brother, Branwell. I fear Robert Heaton is luring him into a web of dangerous secrets."

Harry turned to Emily. "You were right about Branwell. But what could my uncle want with him?"

"Your uncle?" Charlotte said, her thoughts racing. "You're Rachel's missing son?" She stared at him with even more interest. How could she not have noticed that the uncle and nephew shared the same piercing blue eyes?

Harry started. "What do you know about my mother?" His intensity left Charlotte breathless.

"Nothing," she managed to say. "Not since I met her that day on the moors."

"Charlotte!" Emily cried. "You've actually *met* Rachel? Harry wasn't even sure she was still alive!"

"I think it was her . . ." Gratified by their reaction, Charlotte didn't want to disappoint them.

His eyes fixed on Charlotte, Harry ordered, "Describe her."

"Her eyes were blue, like yours. And like Robert Heaton's."

Harry nodded.

"She was beautiful, or had been once. She had reddish-blond hair, with streaks of gray."

"That's my mother!" Harry exclaimed. He pulled at his collar and muttered, "Gray hair? I never should have left her."

"Never mind, Harry," Emily said. "You're here now." She turned to Charlotte. "Why didn't you tell me about this?"

"Heaton told me not to," Charlotte said simply.

"What is your relationship with Heaton? Are you in league with him?" he cried, lunging toward Charlotte.

Emily stepped between them. "Harry, Charlotte would never do anything criminal. She's absurdly righteous."

"Thank you, Emily," Charlotte said waspishly. "Harry, I can assure you I am not working with Heaton. In fact, he quite dislikes me and my meddling ways." Her smile was rueful.

"Charlotte, I don't mean to sound suspicious," Harry said, "but you do see you must tell me everything if I am to trust you?"

"Harry, I already told you . . ." Emily began to defend Charlotte, but Charlotte touched her arm. "It's all right, Em, I don't mind," she said. "I met her by chance on the road from Bradford. She had come from the moor. She stopped my carriage. She spoke so wildly, I feared for her sanity. Then your uncle arrived and took her away."

"Where did he take her?" Harry asked.

Charlotte shook her head. "I've no idea. But on my oath, she was alive less than a week ago. Although . . ." She faltered, recalling her own misgivings.

"What? What aren't you telling me?" Harry demanded.

Slowly she said, "Her wrist, where Heaton grabbed it, was bruised. I wondered at the time if she had been restrained."

"I'll kill him!" Harry vowed, starting toward the path to Ponden Hall.

Emily moved to intercept him. "That won't rescue your mother, which is your first concern."

"Emily, you heard Charlotte. He's tying her up! What else has he done to her? What's to stop him from killing her?"

Charlotte's eyes were wide, and even Emily's face looked pale.

"He wouldn't do such a thing," Emily said, trying to reassure herself as well as Harry.

"I'd lay even odds he had something to do with his father's death. Why not his sister's, too?" Harry ran his fingers through his thick dark hair.

Emily found her voice. "Because it would be too suspicious." She gained confidence as she developed her argument. "There is already talk about your grandfather. If Rachel dies, too, and your uncle is the only one to gain . . . You can see how it looks."

Charlotte couldn't stand to be ignorant any longer. "Emily, you're wading in dark waters—tell me what is happening."

"Charlotte, it's too dangerous," Emily said. "Go home."

"I will not!"

"You should both go home," Harry said. "This is my battle. I'll find my mother. Then I'll take care of my uncle once and for all."

Her shoulders pushed back, Emily said, "Harry, you don't know me very well if you think you can call me off because it might get dangerous."

"Besides, our family is involved now, too," Charlotte said, standing next to her sister. "There are Branwell and Father to think of."

The mist began to turn thicker until it was a drizzle of rain again. Keeper leapt to his feet and nudged Emily toward the tent. "Keeper thinks we should continue this conversation where it is dry," she said.

Harry held the flap open. Charlotte went in first, eyes wide open to take in every detail. She picked up a book from the cot. "Byron?" Charlotte asked. "Small wonder you and Emily are friends."

"Very amusing, Charlotte," Emily said, her arms folded across her chest.

"Please sit down," Harry said. "I apologize the accommodations are not more luxurious."

"I'll begin," Charlotte said, sitting on the cot. "Harry, what does Heaton gain from keeping your mother hidden away?"

"Money. She's inherited half of my grandfather's fortune."

"But isn't he rich enough?" Charlotte asked.

"For some men," Emily said slowly, "there's no such thing as enough."

"He wants capital to expand the mills." Harry scowled.

"Show her what we found today," Emily said.

Harry reached into his satchel and handed Charlotte the papers they had taken from Ponden Hall. She held them close to her nose to read them. Harry flashed an amused glance at Emily, who shook her head with mock disapproval.

"This is your grandfather's will," Charlotte said after a moment. "Where did you get this?" She glared at her sister. "Don't tell me you took this from Ponden Hall?"

"From Heaton's own locked desk drawer," Emily boasted. "I picked the lock!"

Charlotte put her hand to her mouth. "Emily! You stole Heaton's papers? How could you be so reckless?"

"No more reckless than you were when you infiltrated a Freemasons' meeting." Harry said. His admiration was unmistakable, and Charlotte felt a blush creep up her neck to her cheeks. "The next paper is an application to have my mother declared incompetent."

"How cruel!" Charlotte whispered.

"And wicked!" Emily agreed.

"But you're her son," Charlotte said. "You would be in charge of her money, wouldn't you?"

"Harry's been away for years," Emily said. "Perhaps Heaton thinks he's dead."

"He's too sure of himself to risk the whole venture on the chance Harry might be dead." Charlotte shook her head. "There must be more to his plan."

"We found this, too." Emily held up the registry of marriages.

"Bradford parish's missing register?" Charlotte asked. In answer to Emily's questioning look, she said, "Father told me about it."

"Why would Robert have it?" Emily drummed her fingers on the edge of the cot. "It must mean something."

Charlotte read the will a second time. "Your grandfather's will requires any child must be *legitimate*." She stressed the last word.

Emily stared at her sister with admiration. Sometimes Charlotte's maddening insistence on rules and procedures paid unexpected dividends. "Harry, where were your parents married?" Emily asked. "And could you prove the marriage? Do you have a marriage certificate?"

"Of course I don't have their marriage certificate." Harry looked puzzled. "They wed in Bradford, I think."

"Your uncle has the register of marriages for the Bradford parish," Charlotte pointed out. "If he also had taken or destroyed your parents' marriage certificate, you might find it impossible to prove your parents' marriage."

"That's absurd," Harry protested. "Uncle Robert can't just deny something everyone knows to be the truth. What about the priest who performed the ceremony?"

"That would be Reverend Smythe, a close friend of Father's," Charlotte said. "He died two years ago."

"Charlotte, does Harry have any other way to prove he's legitimate?" Emily asked.

Charlotte felt as though she had grown several inches: Emily was asking *her* for advice. She thought for a few moments. "There aren't any other marriage records. But wait: The baptismal record asks for your parents' names. Where were you born?"

"Haworth."

"Father!" Emily and Charlotte said together. Harry looked confused.

"Father would have baptized you," Charlotte explained. "He performs almost all the baptisms in the parish. And he keeps meticulous records."

"Couldn't Robert steal that book, too?" Harry asked.

"He already tried," Emily said to the amazement of the others. "He was the intruder who Father ran off with his pistol. He cut himself on the window."

Charlotte nodded. "I saw the cut on his hand today."

"Might he try again?" Harry asked.

Emily and Charlotte shook their heads. "Father is extremely careful," Charlotte said.

"No one could get near," Emily agreed.

Harry pounded his fist into his hand. "This is not getting us anywhere!"

"Oh!" Charlotte's sudden cry startled both Emily and Harry. "I know what Heaton wants with Branwell. I found some scraps of paper in his room covered with what looked like Father's writing. But what if Branwell was imitating his writing?" She hated to think her own brother could be so wicked.

Emily had no difficulty imagining Branwell as a forger. "Branwell would be very good at it, I would think. Charlotte, what exactly did the scraps of paper say?"

With miserable eyes, she looked from Emily then to Harry. "'Bastard.'"

This scheme I went over twice, thrice;
it was then digested in my mind;
I had it in a clear practical form:
I felt satisfied, and fell asleep.

CHAPTER TWENTY-ONE

$\mathcal{I}$ need some air," Harry said. He walked out into the rain and climbed the hill toward Ponden Hall.

"Harry—" Charlotte started after him, but Emily held her back. "Let him go," she said. "He has an awful lot to think about."

"Should he be alone?" Charlotte turned to look at Emily. "Shouldn't you go to him?"

"Why?" Emily asked sharply. "He's a grown man. He doesn't need me to think for him."

"But . . ."

"*Charlotte.*" Emily gave her sister a shake. "If we want to help Harry, we must devise a plan to rescue Rachel."

Charlotte nodded. Ever since Rachel had stopped her carriage on the road a week ago, she had felt there was a task left undone. A story in need of an ending. But there was another victim to protect. "What about Branwell? He can't fully understand what his involvement with Heaton means. We have to save him, too."

Emily eyed her sister warily, but decided not to argue. "Perhaps we can do both. But first we find Rachel—that's the essential thing. We must do it quickly. Who knows what Heaton has planned?"

"Well, I know where she *was*." Charlotte looked thoughtful. "Rachel was on foot when I met her. She couldn't have come from far away. We just need to find the nearest Heaton property. You can do that easily."

Emily's fingers twisted around each other. "Charlotte, I know I mock you for being practical sometimes . . ."

"Often."

"Often," Emily conceded. "But I have no idea how to find out what property the Heatons own."

"Mr. Greenwood, the stationer, is also Haworth's property clerk. He would help if *you* asked."

Emily was puzzled. "Why would he help me especially?"

"He'd do anything for you." An edge crept into Charlotte's voice. "He's completely smitten with you." Under her breath she added, "Like Harry."

"Charlotte, don't be ridiculous," Emily snapped.

"All you need do is ask."

"Is the shop open on Sunday?" asked Emily.

Charlotte rolled her eyes; Emily never did any errands, so she hadn't the faintest idea of when the shops were open. "He opens in the afternoon on Sundays."

"Fine. I'll ask him," Emily said. "And what will you do?"

"I'll find a way to keep Father's records safe from Branwell." She paused. "That will keep him and Father safe."

Emily glanced up at Harry, silhouetted on the hill. "This is a good plan, Charlotte, because it's up to us. Harry can be emotional," she said, thinking of how he had tossed the valuable book on the fire. "We're more reliable."

Charlotte, to Emily's great surprise, burst out laughing.

━━◆━━

Emily pushed open the door to the stationer's shop, the bell ringing sweetly above her head. The shop was empty except for Mr. Greenwood, looking small behind the battered wooden counter. He straightened up as soon as he saw her and adjusted his sweat-stained collar.

"Hello, Miss Brontë," he said. "You're looking very well today."

"Thank you, Mr. Greenwood," Emily said.

"I saw you walking on the moors a few days ago." His hairless skull was dotted with beads of perspiration.

"I didn't notice you," Emily said. She wondered why he suddenly looked so stricken.

"Are you going to walk today? The weather is clear now, but I heard it's raining a bit to the north."

"Perhaps, after I complete my errands," she said.

"Are you out of writing paper already?" Mr. Greenwood asked anxiously. "I can't get any more until tomorrow."

"We have enough." Emily hurried to reassure him. "Charlotte hasn't begun writing yet. As soon as she does, I'll replenish our stock."

"Then what can I do for you today?"

Emily leaned over the counter. "I heard," she said in a conspiratorial whisper, "you have a record of every piece of property in Haworth."

Mr. Greenwood seemed to stand a little taller. "That's true. Would you like to see my map?" Without waiting for her answer, he disappeared into the back room and came out with a rolled-up map. Emily moved aside the dusty bottles of ink and collections of pen nibs.

With a practiced flick of his wrist, Mr. Greenwood unfurled the map. "It's beautiful!" Emily exclaimed, distracted from her cause by the exquisite detail. Mr. Greenwood had drawn tiny representations of every building. His calligraphy took full advantage of the different-colored inks he had at his disposal. Farms were green, mills blue, and houses carefully drawn in red. The owners or tenants' names were carefully noted.

"You must have studied each building to get such detail," Emily said.

Mr. Greenwood looked gratified and sheepish at the same time. "It's not required, but I like to illustrate my maps. It's by way of being a hobby of mine." He let her admire it for a few moments longer before he asked, "Were you looking for something in particular?"

Emily ran her finger along the road between Bradford and Haworth. "Does the Heaton family own any property near here?" She pointed to the area where Charlotte had met Rachel.

"No, their properties are clustered around Ponden Hall and their mills." Emily must have seemed disappointed because he said, "But they rent a large farm at Top Withins."

"Why? They have plenty of their own, don't they?"

"But Top Withins includes the spring that provides water for their most productive mill. They want to control the water."

Emily stared down at the map. "There are several buildings," she said, thinking how easy it would be to hide one woman. "And it's quite remote, isn't it?"

He nodded emphatically. "It certainly is. And they don't welcome visitors. I stopped by once, just to ask for a glass of water, and I was run off by a vicious dog."

Emily smiled to herself. A dog she could handle. She thanked Mr. Greenwood and turned to leave.

"Must you go?" he asked sadly. "I suppose with illness in the house you need to get home."

She paused at the door. "Illness?"

"I noticed your brother visiting the apothecary's shop across the street."

"When?" Her every sense was on the alert.

"Yesterday."

"Thank you, Mr. Greenwood." Emily bestowed on him a bright smile. "You've no idea how helpful you've been."

He flushed, and stuttered a response, but Emily was already out the door. Picking her way to avoid the sewage flowing freely down the street, she crossed to the apothecary. Emily rarely went there; she didn't trust medicines. And as far as she knew, Branwell had no reason to go there either. Even when her brother had a sore head from overdrinking, their father administered his homemade remedies.

"May I help you, miss?" asked the clerk behind the counter.

"My brother, Mr. Brontë, was in yesterday," she began.

"Are you here to pick up the tonic he ordered?" the clerk interrupted.

Feeling her way, Emily said, "Is it ready?"

"Yes. Tell your brother to be careful with this dosage. It's a stronger concentration than the one I made him a week ago. It's two teaspoons once a day. An overdose can make a patient very confused."

"What's in it?" Emily asked.

"Mostly laudanum in a solution of alcohol."

Laudanum was used for a cough, or to alleviate pain and intestinal problems. Branwell had none of these symptoms. And he certainly didn't need any more alcohol.

Watching her curiously, the clerk added, "And I'll say it again, I wish he would let me put it in the bottle I usually use for medicaments. He had me reuse a harmless tonic bottle—I worry someone might take it in error."

Or be dosed deliberately without their knowledge, Emily thought. "Oh, dear," she said, opening her reticule and pretending to search for money. "I seem to have left home without my wallet. Branwell will have to come by and pick up his tonic after all."

She hurried out and ran up the hill to the parsonage to tell Charlotte what she had discovered. Despite her haste, she slowed when she came to the graveyard. John Brown and his son were digging a new grave. Emily always admired how they dug a grave with the straightest of lines, in proportions just large enough for the recently deceased.

"Who died?" she asked.

"Mrs. Taylor, the seamstress," Brown said without taking his attention away from his digging. "Her heart gave out. The funeral is on Tuesday."

John Brown buried more than a hundred people each year in his perfectly measured graves and marked them with his expertly carved stones. He might as well have been making an entry in her father's register. Name. Occupation. Cause of Death. Add the date, and an entire life was tidied away.

That reminded her of Charlotte's task. She hurried inside the parsonage where Charlotte was arguing with her father in the dining room.

"Charlotte, I appreciate your concern, but I assure you, the parish records are perfectly safe," Rev. Brontë said. He looked up at Emily's entrance. "Hello, dear."

"That's what the priest in Bradford thought, Father," Charlotte answered in her most reasonable voice. "And look what happened there." She and Emily exchanged a quick knowing glance.

"That was a terrible shame." Rev. Brontë looked solemn. "All those records lost. I don't wish to speak ill of the priest there, but he had a sacred duty to protect those records."

"But even your records are only as secure as your study," Charlotte argued. "What harm could there be in locking the registers up?"

"Father, have you forgotten someone tried to break in last week?" Emily added.

Rev. Brontë's face paled. "On second thought, Charlotte, you are correct. There's no sense in taking risks. I'll lock the registers in my cabinet right now."

"Let us help you," Charlotte said, beckoning to Emily to follow him into his study.

"Well done!" Emily whispered to Charlotte as they walked.

The reverend took out his keys and opened his glass cabinet. "I'll put them in here."

"Father, I'll shift them for you," Charlotte offered. "Why don't you finish your tea and I'll bring you the key."

"That's very kind of you, my dear, but I'll do that." He placed all the registers in the cabinet and tucked the key in his waist pocket.

Charlotte shot a dismayed glance at Emily, who shook her head slightly. She took her father's arm and said, "Father, Tabby has an excellent tea waiting for you."

"Thank you, my dear. I must say all the dramatics at church today have given me an appetite."

"I thought your sermon today was inspiring," Emily said, "I was very proud." She hugged her father. Both Rev. Brontë and Charlotte stared at her with surprise. As soon as he was gone, Emily held up the key she had slipped out of their father's pocket.

"You're incorrigible," Charlotte said, beaming. "But how will we get it back to him?"

"He won't believe it if I embrace him again—you'll have to do it!" Emily said.

"Or we could just 'find' it on the floor, and pretend he dropped it." Charlotte unlocked the cabinet and removed the register of births. "Do you know when Harry was born?"

"June fifteenth, eighteen sixteen." She looked at Charlotte sidelong.

"Elizabeth died on June fifteenth," Charlotte said sadly.

"I know."

Blinking away a tear, Charlotte thumbed through the book. "Here it is. Father did baptize him."

Emily held her breath.

"And the record shows his father is Mr. George Casson, husband to Rachel."

Emily exhaled. "Thank goodness. Branwell hasn't changed it yet. We're in time."

"And now the books are locked safely away, Branwell can't hurt himself or Harry." Charlotte breathed a sigh of relief. "How did you fare at Mr. Greenwood's? Do the Heatons own property near that stretch of road?"

"No," Emily said. "But they rent several farms near Top Withins. It's not far from where you met Rachel on the road. It's very remote, a perfect place to hide someone." Emily went to the door to be sure they weren't overheard. "But I found out something else." She told Charlotte about the apothecary.

"Laudanum?" Charlotte asked.

"In an unmarked bottle . . ."

"Rachel!" Charlotte gasped. "That might explain why she acted so very strangely. And as I recall, her pupils were dilated. What if Robert is drugging her to make her appear incompetent or drunk?"

"I wouldn't put it past him. If he had a hand in killing his father, what's drugging his sister compared to that?"

"But why would Heaton have Branwell collect the drug?"

"Heaton is a suspect after his father's accident. He can't afford to be connected with the drug."

"Why would Branwell agree?" Charlotte asked.

Emily waved her hand toward the now-locked-up register. "Who knows why our brother invariably takes the most self-destructive path? Why would he agree to compromise Father's life's work?"

"Altering the register is one thing," Charlotte said. "Robert Heaton could spin him a tale to justify that. But to conspire against an innocent woman? Branwell must be ignorant of what the laudanum is for."

"I don't know," Emily said flatly. "He'd do anything to impress Heaton."

Seeing she wasn't going to convince Emily that Branwell was essentially good, Charlotte pursed her lips. "If it's true, how do we use this information?"

"I thought it might help us find Rachel. When Branwell picks up the medicine, we'll follow him directly to Rachel's location."

Charlotte steepled her fingers and considered. "But what if he just brings it to Robert?"

"Then we'll know to follow Heaton." Emily clasped Charlotte's hand. "It's the quickest way to find her."

Charlotte nodded. "It's a good plan."

Emily said, "I'll get Harry. He needs to be a part of this." But before Emily left the house, she made a stop in her father's bedroom.

Slamming the front door behind her, Emily set off to find Harry. Her father's pistol felt solid and comforting in her skirt pocket.

You say you never heard of a Mrs. Rochester at the
house up yonder . . . but I daresay you have many a
time inclined your ear to gossip about the mysterious
lunatic kept there under watch and ward.

CHAPTER TWENTY-TWO

By the next afternoon, the trap was set. Emily and Harry waited on the moor overlooking Haworth.

"Emily, we must talk," Harry said. "About what happened yesterday." He looked down on Emily, who was seated on a rock beneath a stunted tree. The weather was thick and humid, as though another storm was coming.

"So much happened yesterday," Emily said, her eyes fixed on the graveyard below where Charlotte was hiding and watching for Branwell. The apothecary didn't open until two o'clock, so Branwell couldn't pick up his tonic before then. Once Charlotte spied him, she would signal to Emily and Harry, carefully concealed on the moor path.

"I feel like a complete cad," Harry said. "I never should have kissed you."

"I kissed you first," Emily corrected. "I'm not embarrassed or ashamed. Are you?"

"No, of course not!" He took her hands in his. "But you must be wondering about my intentions."

Emily shook off his hands. "I know your intentions perfectly well. To rescue your mother."

"But what about us?"

"We'll rescue her together," Emily said.

"Damnation, Emily!" he cried. "You are being extremely aggravating—deliberately or not, I cannot decide. Shouldn't we discuss our future?"

Emily took her eyes off the graveyard and gave him her full attention. "I refuse to consider anything beyond this moment."

Harry splayed his hands and then clenched them into fists. His jaw was set, and Emily smiled to herself; she had often seen that same exasperated expression on Charlotte's face.

In the graveyard below, Charlotte's mind swirled with uncharitable thoughts. Emily claimed not to be interested in romance, but somehow she had maneuvered events so Charlotte sat alone on a damp gravestone while Emily waited with the handsome young man with a tragic past. Goodness knew what they were up to without a chaperone.

A door slammed and Branwell came out of the parsonage. Charlotte waved a white cambric handkerchief for Emily to see.

Branwell hurried down the hill to the apothecary. Looking from her brother to her sister, Charlotte's irritation rose anew as Emily made no signal back. "Confound her, she's probably kissing Harry again." After making sure Branwell would not see her, Charlotte stood up and waved her arm wide. Finally, Emily replied with the same signal.

After a short time, Branwell hurried back up the hill, unknowingly passing Charlotte's hiding place. He carried a small package wrapped in brown paper. When he was safely ahead of her, she followed. Hunting quarry was rather exciting, Charlotte thought. Then she recalled Rachel, held against her will, no doubt terrified. This was not a game.

Branwell set a terrific pace, sticking to the path instead of striking out across the waterlogged moors. Harry and Emily waited for Charlotte behind a stand of trees.

"Finally, Charlotte!" Emily exclaimed. "Can't you walk any faster? Branwell is halfway across the moor."

Charlotte scowled, but before she could express her feelings, Harry interrupted. "Never mind; we need to let your brother get ahead of us, anyway."

The three of them took up the chase. Within moments, Harry and Emily were well ahead of Charlotte. The moor was open and empty, so she had no trouble keeping them in sight. Which of course meant if he chanced to look back, Branwell could see them, too. But he never did. It was a point in his favor, Charlotte decided. If he knew he was hurting a defenseless woman, he would be more cautious.

Branwell cut across a wild meadow, his feet getting sucked into the bog. Even the wildflowers hung their heads, they were so drenched. Without hesitation, Harry and Emily followed him into the muck. Many paces back, Charlotte sighed and resigned herself to stepping in water up to her ankles.

Half an hour later, Branwell reached Charlotte's favorite waterfall. It wasn't a great cascade but a series of stone steps, which lowered the water in a soothing murmur.

Although the Brontë siblings had tarried here on many a summer afternoon, Branwell's step did not falter. He crossed the stone bridge and started the steep climb on the other side. Trailing at a safe distance, Emily, Harry, and Charlotte trekked up the hill. Charlotte had rarely explored this part of the moor. But as she matched her mental map with the terrain, she was certain they were walking toward Top Withins. It was a lonely spot, a perfect place to hide a secret.

The sweat trickled down her arms and she could feel the moisture pooling under her bodice. Her sensible boots were beginning to rub at the heels. Then Branwell picked up his already rapid pace; the end of his journey was doubtless in sight.

Briefly silhouetted against the dark sky, Branwell paused at the apex of the moorland path, then plunged down the other side. A few minutes later Harry and Emily reached the crest of the hill and waited for Charlotte to reach them. Charlotte pushed away her fatigue.

"I don't know why you insisted on coming if you couldn't keep up with us," Emily said unkindly.

Charlotte was too breathless to answer immediately. Emily paced impatiently, waiting for Charlotte to regain her breath. Charlotte noticed Emily was keeping her right hand in the pocket of her skirt. Before she could ask why, Harry offered Charlotte a sip of water from a flask.

"Are we at Top Withins?" Charlotte finally gasped.

"We think so," Harry said. "Your brother is trying to attract someone's attention."

Creeping over the crest of the hill, Charlotte looked down at the farm. The main house was tucked into the side of the hill, but there were half a dozen outbuildings. A fence surrounded the house, and a huge, hungry-looking dog stalked its surround. A few trees sheltered the house, but they were deformed and stunted by the constant wind. The air was so thick and still, even the birds were silenced.

"How desolate," Charlotte murmured, thinking the thick dark clouds suited the lonely farm.

"An excellent place to hide someone," Emily said.

Harry's face was stern. "If my mother is there, I'll find her."

Below, Branwell shouted for someone to come out. His small figure with its shock of red hair seemed slightly ridiculous as he approached the fence again and again. Every time, the dog barked viciously, throwing its body at the wooden slats. Much to Emily's amusement, Branwell leapt backward each time it happened.

"Emily, don't laugh," Charlotte scolded. "Not everyone can be fearless around fierce beasts."

Harry gazed at Emily appreciatively. "It takes a special kind of person to befriend a vicious dog," he said.

Charlotte closed her eyes briefly. Harry was completely besotted. Why was it always Emily? Why did no one prize Charlotte's qualities of prudence, responsibility, and virtue?

Below, Branwell's shouts finally received a response. A man came out of a barn. Charlotte recognized the type, a typical dour Yorkshire farmer who would have no patience with idle chitchat. Sure enough, he brushed off Branwell's attempts to start a conversation, taking the parcel Branwell offered and leaving him at the gate.

"There's the tonic," Emily said.

"But where's my mother?" Harry asked.

"Look, Branwell is coming back up the hill. Hide!" They ducked behind a large rock, watching Branwell begin the long trudge home.

"Now what?" Emily asked once their brother was out of view and earshot.

Charlotte watched the weather nervously. The sun was low in the sky and flashes of lightning sparked the copper-colored clouds rolling in on the horizon. It was raining to the north. It wouldn't be long before it reached Top Withins. "I think we should get Father and a constable," she said.

"No!" Emily and Harry spoke together.

"I'm done with waiting," Harry said. "Who knows what my uncle will do next?"

"I agree." Emily nodded. "We need to rescue Rachel now."

Harry started striding toward the house, Emily one step behind.

"Wait!" Charlotte raced forward to stop them. "If you won't wait for a constable, at least do this right. Don't go rushing in willy-nilly."

"You're always too cautious," said Emily.

Charlotte ignored her sister's tone. "Do you have a plan? What about that man we saw? He works for Robert, and he won't just let you take Rachel away."

Harry and Emily exchanged glances, vexing Charlotte again. They're united, she thought, and I'm alone.

"Look, there he is," Harry said. He pointed down to where the hired man had left the house carrying a wooden bucket and trudged to the largest barn.

"Now, we rescue Mother!" Harry raced down the steep path, Emily close on his heels. Charlotte trailed behind.

At the gate, the dog barked and bared his large teeth. Harry stood his ground, just, but Charlotte leapt back as Branwell had done minutes before. "What are we going to do?" she whispered.

"I'll handle this." Emily reached into her pocket and pulled out a small sack full of bones. She began to feed the dog through the slats.

"Where . . ." Charlotte began.

"Let's just say Tabby's soup may be a bit thin tonight." Emily grinned. "Mr. Greenwood mentioned a vicious dog, and I thought we could use an advantage."

"He's licking your hand." Harry stared at Emily with approval.

"He's not the only one," Charlotte muttered.

"You two go to the door," Emily whispered. "I'll tie the dog up behind the house."

A moment later, Harry was knocking on the kitchen door. All houses on the moors are the same, Charlotte thought. No matter how grand the front door, entry is almost always easier at the kitchen. And so it proved. A tiny elderly woman opened the door.

With an exclamation of delight, Harry stooped down and embraced the woman in a warm hug. "Hannah!"

"Is that young Harry?" A curious mixture of disbelief and dismay crossed the old woman's features.

Harry turned to Charlotte and Emily, who had rejoined them. "Hannah was my nursemaid." He embraced the woman again, his height dwarfing her tiny frame. "I've been searching for her."

"Mister Harry, we thought you were dead," Hannah said, dashing tears from her cheeks.

"I'm very much alive," Harry assured her. "But where is Mother? Is she here? Is she well?"

"She's well enough, considering . . ." Hannah's voice trailed off.

Harry placed his hands on her shoulders. "Take me to her, Hannah!" Charlotte admired his restraint. She had rather thought he would have pushed past the old lady and started searching.

"I'm not supposed to bring her any visitors," Hannah said, wringing her apron.

"Visitor?" Harry cried. "I'm her *son*!"

Her face distressed, Hannah said, "I'll lose my position if I disobey the master. And who would hire an old woman like me?" Tears rolling down her wrinkled cheeks, she said, "Mister Harry, don't ask it of me!"

"I don't have much time!" Harry glanced back toward the barn.

"Harry, let me." Charlotte stepped forward so Hannah could see her. "Hannah, do you know me? I'm the Reverend Brontë's daughter."

"Yes, miss." Hannah's eyes darted from Harry to Charlotte.

"This is my sister," Charlotte said indicating Emily. "We're here to bring Mrs. Casson to the parsonage."

"We don't call her that anymore," Hannah whispered. "She's Miss Rachel now. Mister Harry, Misses Brontës—she's not well. The Master thinks her mind might be going."

Harry's face darkened.

"All the more reason she needs her son," Charlotte said, placing her hand on Harry's muscular forearm to restrain him.

"Let us in, you silly woman!" Emily cried.

Glaring at Emily, Charlotte put her arm around Hannah and led her away from the door into the large kitchen. The ceilings were low and a large fireplace took up one whole side of the room.

Charlotte sat Hannah down on a bench against the wall. "Do you want to be responsible for keeping Miss Rachel and her son apart? What if it's his absence that turned her brain?"

"Oh, Miss Charlotte, I don't know what to think." Hannah grabbed Charlotte's hand. "I practically raised that boy, but the master says terrible things about him!"

Harry moved about the spacious kitchen like a caged animal. He began searching the rooms adjacent to the kitchen. Emily perched on the back of a settee, her eyes fixed on him as though she was memorizing every detail of his distress.

Hannah's eyes also followed Harry's every movement. Charlotte had to snap her fingers in front of Hannah to get her attention. "Did you believe what Mr. Robert said?"

Hannah shook her head. "I never did."

Charlotte squeezed Hannah's hand. "And you were right. Harry is here to help his mother. Won't you let him see her?"

"I don't know, miss!" Hannah wailed.

"Of course you do. Aren't you a decent, God-fearing woman? One of my father's parishioners? You'll do the right thing. Is she upstairs?"

Hannah was sobbing now, but in between her heaving breaths, she nodded. "She's locked in for her own protection."

Furious, Harry was about to run up the stairs when he heard Charlotte ask, "Do you have the key?" He froze, waiting for Hannah's answer.

Hannah reached into her deep pocket and pulled out an iron key. Emily darted forward and snatched it from her hands, and she and Harry bounded up the back stairs.

"Miss Brontë," Hannah whispered. "My master comes every day to give his sister her medicine."

"He cares so much about her welfare, does he?" Charlotte asked drily.

"He visits as regular as winter in December." Hannah's eyes were fixed on the clock hanging on the wall.

A sinking feeling in her stomach, Charlotte understood Hannah's warning. "When?"

"Always at sunset."

A glance out the window told Charlotte the bad news. They had very little time.

Then her ears finally registered a distant noise that had been steadily growing louder. It was the thudding of hooves. Charlotte rushed to the door and saw Robert Heaton riding up to the house.

"Run upstairs and tell Harry his uncle is here!" Charlotte turned to Hannah. "I will deal with Mr. Heaton."

Hannah hesitated.

"Hannah, what will happen if Mr. Heaton finds Harry with Miss Rachel?"

"I'll warn them," Hannah said, and rushed upstairs. Charlotte straightened up and steeled herself. No matter the cost, she must purchase enough time for Emily and Harry to rescue Rachel.

Charlotte waited until Robert had tied his horse to a post near the stable. He wore tight riding breeches and a fine green riding coat. She met him on the gravel path leading from the house to the barn.

"You!" He stared at her in consternation. "What are you doing here?" He carried a riding crop he impatiently slapped against his leg.

"Good day, Mr. Heaton."

"Answer me, Miss Brontë." He looked down his long nose at her, his beard like an arrow piercing her breast. "Why are you trespassing on my property?"

"Surely it's not trespassing to knock on the door." Charlotte forced herself to laugh lightly, as though she found his question the most amusing thing in the world. "I heard your sister was still unwell and I felt it was my Christian duty to pay a visit."

"Who told you she was here?" He glanced at the house.

Barely hesitating, Charlotte decided to drive a wedge between Robert and her brother. "Why, Branwell, of course."

Without taking his eyes from her face, he shouted over his shoulder at the wildly barking dog. "Shut up, you cur!" Glowering at Charlotte, he said, "I don't believe it!"

"Really?" Charlotte asked, conscious that every word she spoke bought Emily a little more time. "How else would I know the apothecary mixes a special tonic you administer each evening?"

Robert gaped at her and swayed a little as though she had thrown him off-balance. He shook himself and started to walk past her.

"An odd tonic, to be sure," Charlotte went on, catching at his sleeve. "It seems to make your sister terribly confused. One might wonder if it was filled with opiates!"

"You've spoken to her?" he asked, turning around, his brows drawn together in a fierce scowl.

She tore her eyes from his face, suffused with rage, and kept a sharp watch on his clenched fists. Her next volley was sure to push him over the edge of good sense.

"Don't worry; she is in excellent hands." Charlotte took a deep breath. "Her son is with her." She braced herself for an explosion.

Instead he said in a flat, angry voice, "The bastard?"

"I wouldn't count on that, Mr. Heaton. Harry can prove he is legitimate." She lifted her gaze to see the inevitable dismay on his face. "You've lost."

Heaton snapped without warning. With a roar, he slashed at her head with his riding crop. The crop cut into her forehead and she fell to the ground. Dizzy from the blow, she lay in the gravel, watching helplessly as he burst into the house.

She clambered to her feet and touched her hand to her head. Blood seeping through her fingers, she stumbled toward the house.

CHAPTER TWENTY-THREE

A few minutes earlier, Harry had bounded up the uneven wooden stairs, Emily close behind. They paused at the landing, staring at the three doors. Only one was shut. Harry tried the handle; it was locked. Wordlessly, Emily handed him the key.

The door swung open to reveal a small, dark room. Even though it was not yet dusk, the curtains were drawn and a small oil lamp glowed dimly. The only furniture was a narrow bed and a rickety chair. A woman was huddled under a blanket. She peered out, blinking at whoever was invading her privacy.

"Mother!" Harry cried, rushing to embrace her. She wore a dressing gown and her feet were bare. Her red hair hung around her shoulders.

"Is that you, Harry? Has my son come back to me?" Rachel began sobbing. "I thought you were dead! I was all alone."

"Mother, I'm here." Emily saw the guilt on his face. He had run away to save himself—but his mother had borne the cost. "I'm going to get you out of here."

Emily stepped into the room. Rachel recoiled. "Who is that?"

"This is my friend." Harry tightened his arm around his mother's shoulders. "You remember Rev. Brontë's daughter, Emily?"

Rachel tilted her head and studied Emily for a moment. "Harry, she's tricking you. This isn't the reverend's daughter. She was a little girl with her nose in a book."

Over Rachel's head, Emily met Harry's stricken gaze.

"Hello, Mrs. Casson." Emily greeted her gently. "I used to be little, but I've grown up since then." She tugged on Harry's arm. "We must get her away from here. Once we're in town, my father can protect her."

Emily noticed Rachel's hair was clean, as was her person. She might be a prisoner, but Hannah took good care of her. She looked around for Rachel's shoes.

There was a thudding of steps coming up the stairs. Hannah burst into the room. "The master is here! Miss Charlotte is outside trying to delay him."

"We're out of time," Emily cried. "Where are her shoes, Hannah?"

"The master made me hide them after she ran away last time." She saw Emily's horrified expression and said quickly, "I'll get them!"

"Did you hear, Emily? Uncle Robert took away her shoes. She's a prisoner." Harry's jaw was set and his hands were forming into fists. "I'll kill him for what he's done."

"Harry, the most important thing is to save your mother!" Emily cried.

"My mother will only be safe when my uncle is no longer a threat," Harry said. "But you're right. First we have to get her to a safe place." He wrapped his mother's white shawl around her shoulders.

Hannah appeared, holding Rachel's shoes. She and Emily knelt at Rachel's bare feet and began lacing.

From below, they heard Charlotte cry out a desperate warning. It was too late. Robert Heaton stormed up the stairs and filled the doorway. Harry leaped up to stand between Robert and Rachel. Emily was struck by the resemblance between the furious men.

"So you've come crawling back," Robert said. "I suppose it's been you sneaking around Ponden Hall like a thief?"

"I'm not here to fight with you," Harry said through gritted teeth. "I'm here to take my mother away."

"I think not. She's unwell," Robert said, an immovable object. "Hannah, tell him."

Tying Rachel's laces, Hannah said, "It's true. Mr. Heaton has a doctor come to see her every week."

"Another Mason, no doubt," Harry spat out.

"You're not needed here, nephew," Robert said. "I'll have the law on you for trespassing."

"You've betrayed us all for money," Harry said with a snarl. "I wouldn't be surprised if you had a hand in Grandfather's death. Not that I cared for the old man. But to kill him? For what? Money?"

"That's a lie!" Robert jabbed a finger at Harry's chest. As though Robert had burst a blister of anger and hate, Harry pulled back his right arm and landed a punch on his uncle's chin. Robert stumbled back, then, like a bull, dropped his shoulder and charged Harry. His momentum carried them both into the wall.

Emily shouted, "Watch out, Harry!"

Rachel began screaming, a high-pitched, terrified noise.

"Mr. Robert, Mr. Harry! Oh, stop!" Hannah cried. "You're upsetting Miss Rachel!" She covered her own eyes and began to sob.

Harry pushed back from the wall and clawed at Robert's coat, pulling it over his uncle's shoulders and pinning his arms for just long enough for Harry to slip out from Robert's grip. To Emily, Harry shouted, "Take my mother!"

"What about you?" she cried.

"I have unsettled business. Go!"

Emily pulled Rachel toward the door; she couldn't take her eyes from the two men fighting. Robert ripped off his coat and began pummeling Harry in the stomach. Winded, Harry slumped against the wall.

Moving more quickly than Emily anticipated, Heaton lunged for Rachel. He grabbed Rachel's arm and tried to pull her away from Emily and the safety of the door.

"No!" cried Emily. "Harry, help!"

Emily struggled to hold on to Rachel in this life-or-death tug-of-war, but Robert was too strong for her. Instinctively she let go entirely and Rachel fell forward into his arms.

Emily took her father's pistol from her pocket. She leveled it at the exact center of Robert's chest. "Release her, Mr. Heaton. Now." If Emily's voice trembled, her shooting hand did not.

Heaton's eyebrows lifted high as he saw the gun. "You don't have the nerve."

Emily took aim at a mirror hanging on the wall behind him. He turned around to see the scene reflected in the cloudy surface. Emily squeezed the trigger and shot his reflection dead in the center of his forehead. Splinters of glass flew everywhere. A tiny shard cut Harry's cheek. Rachel and Hannah shrieked with terror. Heaton was made of sterner stuff, but he paled.

Harry pushed himself away from the wall and pulled the glass from his face. "She has more than enough nerve," he panted.

"Let Mrs. Casson go," Emily repeated. "Or your leg will be next. Or perhaps your head. I'm a good shot."

Robert slowly unhanded his sister.

"Thank you," Emily said. She pulled Rachel behind her. Walking backward, Emily's pistol unwaveringly aimed at Robert's heart, they moved toward the doorway. "Hannah," Emily said. "Come help us with Mrs. Casson."

"My shawl," Rachel said, reaching for where it had fallen to the floor. For a split second, Emily took her attention from Heaton, who lunged at Rachel, pulling her out of Emily's grasp. Harry shouted and dove at his uncle's legs, loosening his uncle's grip.

Emily pulled Rachel out of harm's way, but Harry and Robert, fighting as if their lives were at stake, blocked the doorway. The women backed into the corner.

Robert threw Harry against the table. With a crack, the rickety table collapsed, sending the oil lamp crashing to the floor. Within seconds, oil pooled all around. A lick of flame touched the oil briefly, then suddenly the flame was everywhere. The fire leapt to the curtains and began to travel, quick as lightning, around the room. In moments, the room was filled with smoke.

Harry and his uncle were still rolling about the floor, pummeling each other, oblivious to the flames around them. Rachel and Hannah cowered on the floor, shrieking, while Emily thought furiously.

"For God's sake, stop screaming!" Emily shouted. She stuck the pistol back in her pocket and wrapped the pale shawl about Rachel's head, leaving some fabric to cover her mouth. She did the same with Hannah's apron. "Breathe through the fabric."

She took a strong grip on Rachel's waist with one hand and grabbed Hannah with the other and held her breath. She propelled them both through the fire to the now open doorway. Emily spared a fleeting moment to wish she had more time to fix the sensation of passing through flame in her memory.

"Harry, save yourself!" Emily shouted. "I'll take care of your mother!" Half carrying, half pushing Rachel, Emily made it down the stairs. Hannah, shaking, recalled herself to her duties and began to minister to her mistress. At that moment, Charlotte stumbled into the kitchen, her eyes glassy and a cut bleeding profusely across her forehead.

"Charlotte!" Emily took one look at her sister and grabbed a clean cloth from the table.

"Where's Harry?" Charlotte asked.

"Upstairs, fighting with Robert." Emily wadded up the cloth and pressed it to Charlotte's cut. "There's a fire. Get Rachel and Hannah somewhere safe." She paused. "Can you do that?"

The moment Charlotte nodded, Emily grabbed a ewer full of water.

"Emily! Where are you going?

"To save Harry!"

Robert was unconscious in the hallway. Harry must have dragged him out. In the bedroom, Harry had pulled the burning curtains to the center of the room and was stomping out the flames. Emily poured the water over the smoldering mattress.

"My mother?" Harry asked, his back to Emily, his voice strained.

"She's fine," Emily assured him. "Charlotte is with her." When he didn't turn around, she touched him on the shoulder. "Harry?"

He turned slowly and she gasped. His face was a ruin of blisters and burns. She had escaped with Rachel, but Harry had paid the price.

He held out his hands to her and she saw that they were blackened. Emily let herself recognize the unmistakable odor of burnt flesh. Harry saw the reflection of his injuries in her eyes and his legs gave out beneath him. She caught him, stumbling under the dead weight. She wrapped his arm around her shoulder and somehow got him into the fresher air in the hallway. Turning her head, she shouted, "Charlotte! I need you. But don't let Rachel come up!"

Charlotte came running, compelled by the urgency in Emily's voice. "What is it?" Her voice trailed off. "Oh my goodness," she gasped.

"He needs to lie down."

Charlotte opened a door and found another bedroom. Together they lowered Harry onto a cotton mattress without blankets or bedding.

"We have to get a doctor," Charlotte said. "These burns need bandaging. And as soon as the shock wears off, he's going to be in terrible pain."

Harry mumbled something incomprehensible. Steeling herself, Emily came in close to his raw lips to listen.

"He wants us to get his mother to safety," she said.

"But what about Heaton?" Charlotte pointed to Robert's body in the hall.

Emily perched on the edge of the bed and put her head in her hands. After a moment, she looked up at her sister. "Our first duty is to Rachel. It's what we agreed, and it's what Harry wants."

"And Harry?"

"Wait." Emily ran down the stairs and found Hannah soothing Rachel on the stone steps outside the kitchen. "Her tonic. Where is it?"

"What? I don't understand!" Hannah moaned.

"Look, old woman," Emily said harshly. "That boy you raised is half burned to death."

"What happened to my son?" Rachel began to scream and sob at the same time.

Hannah too began to cry, but Emily was relentless. "Where's the tonic? He's going to be in horrendous pain without it."

"But Miss Rachel's tonic is harmless," Hannah protested.

"It's full of opiates," Emily snapped.

Rachel moaned and began to frantically pull at her hair and clothes.

"Harry needs it *now*," Emily said. "Where is it?"

Hannah pointed to the kitchen table. Emily grabbed the bottle and a wooden spoon and hurriedly gave Rachel a large dose. Hannah's eyes were wide. Emily raced back upstairs to Harry and Charlotte.

"Will that help him?" Charlotte asked. "Are you certain?"

"Laudanum will keep the pain at bay until we can return with a doctor." She poured a dose into the spoon and gently, ever so gently, pried open his mouth and tipped the spoon empty. She did it again until his breathing slowed and his body sought the oblivion of sleep.

"Have you told his mother?"

"She's practically in a stupor," Emily retorted without explaining how Rachel got that way. "Time enough to tell her when we have better news."

"Perhaps we should give Heaton some tonic, too," Charlotte suggested in a low voice. "To keep him unconscious and no trouble to anybody."

Emily shot Charlotte an amused look. "We need to keep it in case Harry needs more."

Charlotte nodded and they returned to the kitchen. Charlotte beckoned to Hannah and explained she needed to stay with Harry until the doctor arrived. "Lock the door. Heaton may wake and I don't want him to hurt Harry any more."

"Miss, will there never be an end to the boy's suffering?" Hannah asked. "His childhood was full of pain. And now this!"

"He's sleeping now; just keep watch," Charlotte instructed.

"We'll send a doctor as soon as we can. We're taking Rachel to our father at the parsonage," Emily said. Hannah nodded mutely. "I don't know if Robert will ever wake, but I intend to be home before he does." She turned to her sister. "Let's go."

Charlotte pointed to Rachel. "She's in no condition to walk across the moor."

"You're right. And I don't like that cut on your forehead; I don't want you to walk either," Emily said, gnawing on a fingernail. "We need a horse and cart or buggy."

"I know there's at least one horse," Charlotte said. "Robert rode in on one."

"There's bound to be a cart we can hitch it to," Emily said.

"We don't have much time before Robert awakes," Charlotte warned.

"Then we'll have to hurry."

Self-abandoned, relaxed, and effortless, I seemed to
have laid me down in the dried-up bed of a great
river; I heard a flood loosened in remote mountains,
and felt the torrent come; to rise I had no will, to flee
I had no strength. I lay faint, longing to be dead.

CHAPTER TWENTY-FOUR

hat are you doing?" It was the dour farmhand, holding a pitchfork aimed at Emily. "Who are you?"

Emily pointed her pistol at him and said, "I'm borrowing this cart. Please harness a horse for me." Staring at the pistol, the man did as she asked.

"Thank you," Emily said sweetly. "Your employer may have use for you in the house. There's been a fire." He backed out of the barn and made himself scarce.

Outside, Charlotte was watching the clouds nervously as she sat on the step, propping Rachel against her as best she could.

Top Withins had an excellent view across the moors, and she could see a massive rainstorm moving quickly across the land. A look of relief appeared on her face when she saw the cart.

"Why not Robert's horse?" Charlotte asked. "Wouldn't it be quicker?"

"That one isn't for a cart. He's never been trained to it," Emily said confidently. "We wouldn't get a mile before he'd rear up and kick the traces."

"You're never wrong about animals," Charlotte said. "We'll need a lantern, too. Take Rachel." When she returned with a lantern, Emily was settling a sleepy Rachel into the back of the cart. Emily had arranged a layer of horse blankets for Rachel's bed, with another blanket on top to keep her warm.

Within minutes, Charlotte had the reins while Emily steadied Rachel. The cart lurched along the rutted road. Large raindrops splattered on the already sodden road in front of them.

"Charlotte, could you possibly hit any more mud holes in the road?" Emily called out. "Rachel will bounce onto the road if you keep driving like this."

"Do you want to drive?" Charlotte, hunched over the reins, peered into the twilight. "This is hard enough without quarreling." The rain had picked up and their dresses were soaked through.

"Look, there's the bridge up ahead. We're not too far from home." The bridge spanned a small tributary of a river from the Crow Hill bog, looming off to the left of the road. Crow

Hill was placed higher than any other part of the moor, and several rivers emanated from it.

Suddenly the horse veered to one side and lurched to a stop. In the same instant there was a distant explosion.

"Emily!" Charlotte screamed. The frantic horse tossed its head and reared between the cart rails. The reins were ripped from Charlotte's hands. "He's going to bolt!"

Emily was already out of the cart, trying to pull the horse's head down. "Shush, quiet, boy," she murmured. As though her touch alone could soothe him, the animal calmed. He still moved uneasily, but he was no longer poised to run.

"What was that?" Charlotte asked as Emily climbed back in. She squinted, trying to see in the growing darkness.

"I don't know. Listen, there's something else," Emily said. She pointed above and in front of them, to the head of the narrow river where it cascaded from Crow Hill. The water, already running high, became a rushing torrent. A rumble made the ground shake. "It's all the rain! The bog has burst!"

Rocks began to fly down the riverbed. At the mouth of the river, Charlotte saw a wall of mud and stone, tipping headlong down the riverbed. Its path was perpendicular to the road they were taking. Charlotte stared, frozen, unable to comprehend that the river could turn so deadly so quickly.

"Charlotte, we have to move!" Emily cried as she jumped in the cart beside Charlotte. "It's going to take out the bridge and we'll have no way home!"

"But . . ."

"Fly!"

Infected by Emily's urgency, Charlotte commanded the horse to move. When he balked, she slapped his rump with the trailing end of the rein.

"Faster!" Emily shouted.

They were racing the tons of rock and water to the bridge. The cart rattled over the stone bridge, and seconds later the torrent hit the bridge.

Charlotte pulled up on the other side, a safe distance from the water. She and Emily turned to watch the scene. The ancient stone supports shifted and groaned. The arch of the bridge buckled under the impact. Half of it was torn away by the onslaught.

Emily stood up in the cart, facing the river. Transfixed by the sight, her mouth hung half open and she sniffed the air, breathing in deeply the scent of mud and dislodged stone.

Charlotte pulled at her arm. "Emily, sit down. It's over."

As if being recalled from a dream, Emily blinked and gradually her eyes focused on Charlotte's face. "Yes, let's go home." She let Charlotte pull her back down to the seat.

Charlotte urged the horse forward. Emily turned her head to watch the river as long at it was in view. "This river feeds the Ponden Mills. It'll be polluted for months," Emily murmured. "They'll be shut down until the water drains." She shrugged. "It serves Robert Heaton right."

Raising her eyebrows, Charlotte said, "And what about all his workers? They don't deserve to be out of work. Emily, your ideas of revenge are too selfish."

Charlotte waited for the inevitable tart reply, but Emily surprised her with an unexpected smile.

"Dear Charlotte, that is why I have you. You are my practicality and my conscience."

"Humph," Charlotte said with a sniff.

It was completely dark before they arrived in Haworth. Emily was thankful Charlotte had thought of putting a lantern on the cart. Charlotte zigged and zagged up Haworth's steep main street. The flagstones that paved the street were placed crosswise to give better traction for the horse's feet, but still the carriage tended to slip backwards if Charlotte wasn't vigilant.

"It feels so late," Charlotte said.

Emily nodded. "But look—the pubs are filled with people. It's not as late as we think."

"Is Rachel still asleep?" Charlotte asked.

"Laudanum is a wonderful thing," Emily said.

"Emily! You drugged her?"

Emily shrugged. "You must admit this has been an easier journey without her sobbing and screeching all the time."

Since that was true, Charlotte contented herself with pressing her lips together in a disapproving line.

They passed the apothecary and the stationer's. Charlotte shivered when looking down Newall Street, where the Three Graces Lodge was situated. As they crested the hill, just before the parsonage was in sight, Charlotte pulled over.

Emily asked, "What's wrong?"

Charlotte hesitated, then said, "I've the oddest feeling that danger awaits us."

"We left all the danger behind at Top Withins," Emily said scornfully. "We have no time for your premonitions. The sooner we drop off Rachel, the sooner we can get Harry a doctor."

"Don't you think I know the urgency?" Charlotte asked with asperity. "But I think you should go ahead to the parsonage and make sure it's safe."

"Heaton is unconscious at Top Withins. He couldn't have sent a message to anyone." But Emily climbed down from the cart. "I've never seen you act like this."

"I've felt like this once or twice before," Charlotte said, remembering her trepidation when Emily was so ill at school. "I've learned not to ignore it."

Emily considered Charlotte and finally nodded with decision. "I'll go look." Without waiting for Charlotte to object, she set off. Hugging the walls of the stores on the corner, Emily edged her way to get a view of the parsonage. In moments she came running back.

"Heaton's there waiting for us!" she whispered. "Charlotte, your little feeling just saved Rachel's life!"

"He must have woken up and ridden his horse like the devil to beat us here."

Emily agreed. "I suspect he saw the bog burst and took his horse across the moors. It's dangerous, but it can be done."

"Should we find a constable?" Charlotte asked.

"The nearest one is in Bradford," Emily replied.

"What about Father's other deacons?"

"We don't know who's a Freemason and who isn't," Emily pointed out. "Anyway, why not just drive up to the gate? What can Robert do to us in front of our father's house?"

"He's been pushed very far today. He's definitely furious—maybe even a little insane." Charlotte shook her head sharply. "I don't think we should chance it. He might be armed." She shivered. "But there's no other way to get home."

"Not by cart," Emily said. "I know a way to approach the parsonage from the church side without Robert seeing. But I have to go on foot."

"What about me and Rachel?"

"I'll lure Robert away from the gate so you can get in safely."

"No." Charlotte was adamant. "It's too dangerous. We'll do it together."

Emily looked at Charlotte for a long moment. "You know, I've misjudged you. You really are quite brave."

"While I think *you* are as reckless as ever," Charlotte retorted, but she could feel the heat in her cheeks. It was seldom indeed Emily paid her a compliment and now three times in one night.

"You must stay with Rachel. When it's safe, I'll hoot like an owl. They're a nocturnal bird; Robert won't even notice."

Charlotte nodded. "All right. But be careful."

Before Emily left, she handed Charlotte her pistol.

"I knew you had something you didn't want me to see," Charlotte said. "You must be mad. You don't even know how to use that thing."

Emily was uncharacteristically silent.

"When did you learn to shoot?" Charlotte accused.

"Father taught me while you were away," Emily admitted. "The pistol is his. Give it back to him. He might need it, especially if Branwell is home."

The awful possibility Branwell might choose Robert Heaton over his own sisters reduced Charlotte to silence. Emily slipped away into the darkness.

We've braved its ghosts often together,
and dared each other to stand among the graves
and ask them to come. But, Heathcliff, if I dare
you now, will you venture? . . . I'll not lie there by
myself; they may bury me twelve feet deep . . .
I won't rest till you are with me.

CHAPTER TWENTY-FIVE

*E*mily edged along the side of the church, hidden from Robert Heaton's line of sight. Her stomach was suddenly roiling. Who was she to dare face him alone? Breathing deeply, she tried to summon the courage she had always taken for granted before. A thick fog floated down from the moor like an ancient army of wraiths. Emily imagined her dear departed sisters there, guarding her and giving her the strength to be brave.

Aware that with every second she hesitated, she risked Charlotte losing her patience and doing something foolish,

Emily scanned the graveyard she knew so well. She soundlessly clambered over the wall farthest away from the parsonage. Her long skirt caught on a sharp rock that ripped a hole in the fabric. Rather than waste time freeing herself, Emily ripped the bottom of the skirt clean away. Luckily, she didn't have too many petticoats to hinder her movement.

Standing inside the graveyard, Emily lay her hand on a gravestone and quickly lifted it in surprise. Instead of cold, damp stone, she felt wet cloth. She looked closer. Her father was in a constant battle with the town's washerwomen, who used the tombstones to dry their laundry. One of them had forgotten her sheet in this remote corner. As Emily fingered the white fabric, an idea took shape.

Sheet in hand, she clambered up the stunted tree at the graveyard's edge and tied the sheet to the lowest branch. A few more judicious knots and some rather clever draping, and the hanging sheet resembled a figure shrouded in a white robe or shawl.

After dropping to the ground, Emily took a deep breath. Then she cupped her hand to her mouth. "Rachel, be careful," she called out in a voice loud enough to be heard at the graveyard's far reaches. "Don't trip, dear."

She paused as though her companion had responded. In an even louder voice she pretend-replied, "Oh, no, my dear Rachel. There's no need to worry. We're almost there. You've been very brave."

In the gloom by the gate, she saw movement and then heard purposeful footsteps in her direction. Heaton was already well inside the graveyard when Emily heard him stumble on a sunken tombstone and curse loudly. She could see his outline a stone's throw from her hiding place.

"Rachel! Is that you?" he called, his voice reason itself. "I've been so worried." Although he spoke calmly, he quickly moved forward. He reached the tree and grabbed the sheet. "Now I've got you." It fluttered to the ground and he realized he had been fooled. "Damnation!" he growled.

"Such language, and on sanctified ground!" Emily mocked him from behind a large stone table that also served as a gravestone. Her voice echoed about the graveyard.

She darted farther into the center of the graveyard, where the tombstones were most crowded. Flitting from one row to another, she easily avoided the stones half-buried in the ground.

"Miss Brontë? Emily, I'm guessing. Your sister is too prim to try such a stratagem."

"You might be surprised by what Charlotte is capable of," Emily said.

"Why don't you show yourself?" Heaton asked. Emily could hear the strain in his voice as he tried to control his temper. "Once I explain my sister's condition, you will see you have completely misunderstood the situation. Come out and we'll discuss it." He was trying to follow her but lacked her knowledge of the terrain.

"I think not," she said. "I've seen how you treat those who cross you." She ducked under a table grave marker and had to stop short, wheeling her arms to keep from falling into the open grave John Brown had dug only the day before. She recovered herself and a plan formed itself in her mind.

Heaton said, "You mean my so-called nephew?" His shape moved toward her, but not quite far enough.

"Yes, your sister's legal heir. Harry has told me everything." Emily deliberately stepped into a clear patch of night, the fog framing her like a painting.

"I see you now, you little minx. You've nowhere to run," Heaton said, his eyes darting around the dark graveyard. "Where is Rachel?"

"I'll never tell," she said.

As she had hoped, Heaton rushed forward to grab her. But Emily had lured him well. His momentum almost carried him across the hole just the right size for a coffin. As he plummeted, his hand caught the edge of her ragged skirt.

"Let go!" Emily clawed at his hand, but it was no use: Heaton was pulling her down with him. "Let me go!" she shouted again.

As the tattered fabric ripped away, Heaton was thrown into the grave. There was an awful crack.

"My ankle—it's broken!" he shouted.

Emily gathered up her skirts. "Are you sure?" She peered into the hole.

Heaton was lying in the dirt, grasping his ankle. Even from her viewpoint, she could see it was swelling up.

"For God's sake, get a doctor!" he snarled.

"I would, Mr. Heaton, except he is needed to minister to your nephew. You'll have to wait," Emily said, watching him struggle with no little satisfaction. The grave was deep and there were six inches of water at the bottom, so Heaton's feet had no purchase even if his ankle was sound.

She hooted three times.

"I won't stand for this!" Heaton cried. "I'll ruin your father and I'll ruin you!"

"Hush," Emily said. "Hoot. Hoot." She listened but heard nothing. "Hoot. Hoot."

She sighed with relief when her keen ears heard the wheels of the cart, then the familiar squeak of the gate. She put one hand on a tall gravestone and trembled, allowing herself finally to experience all the terror she had carefully bottled up until her part was done. Rachel and Charlotte were safe. She had done it—Heaton was no longer a threat to any of them.

A loud bark came from the parsonage garden. Keeper, looking like a mythical creature of darkness, bounded to the top of the wall. His noble head sniffed the air and came running to Emily in the graveyard. He nuzzled Emily's hand. She hugged him, drawing strength from the massive dog.

"You witch!" Heaton wasn't finished with his threats. "I'll have the law on you if you don't get me out right now!"

Keeper's tail stopped wagging and he stepped toward the grave, looked down, and growled. Heaton fell silent.

"Good boy, Keeper," Emily said. "I'd rather not attract too much attention until I've talked to Father."

The door to the sexton's house opened, spilling out a pool of light. "Who's there?" John Brown's stentorian voice called out.

"Too late," Emily muttered.

A moment later Brown, his nightshirt hastily tucked into his trousers, approached the graveyard, his son in tow, carrying a lantern.

"What's going on here?" he called. He stopped short when he saw Emily. "Miss Brontë, I heard voices," he said. "Is anything the matter?"

"Mr. Heaton has stumbled into a grave," Emily said, not forgetting for a moment that John Brown was not only her father's employee but also the Worshipful Master of the Three Graces Lodge. Her hand dropped to Keeper's broad forehead.

Brown's son leaned over the grave and held up the lantern to peer in.

"Mr. Heaton?" The boy's voice was unbelieving. From Heaton in his grave, the boy looked to Emily with wide eyes that looked black in the lantern light.

"Get me out! This madwoman shoved me in here!" Heaton shouted. "She broke my ankle."

"Robert, I'll get you out!" Brown called, keeping a wary eye on the dog. "Son, get the ladder." The boy placed the lantern on a gravestone and obediently loped away.

"Before you do, Mr. Brown," Emily said, "you might ask how Mr. Heaton came to be chasing me through a graveyard in the middle of the night."

"Chasing *you?*" Brown's eyes became as wide as his son's. "Miss Emily, tell me everything that has happened. There is more at stake here than you realize."

"I doubt your stakes are higher than mine," Emily said. "He was threatening my life, after all." Brown stared at her.

"She's a lunatic. Brown, get me out of here." Heaton shouted from the grave.

"Don't you think you ought to consult my father? I think it very likely he will be summoning a constable to place Mr. Heaton under arrest."

"Arrest?" Brown was shocked. For the first time, Emily considered the possibility that his role in all this was innocent. "What are you accusing him of doing, Miss Emily?"

"Don't listen to any of her lies, Brown. Get me out of here!" Heaton's voice was hoarse from his shouting.

Emily had known John Brown since she was a babe; she decided to give him the benefit of the doubt. She drew him away from the grave and spoke in a low voice. "Kidnapping, to start."

"Who?" Brown asked uneasily.

"His own sister. He kept her prisoner at Top Withins and drugged her."

"She wasn't kidnapped," Brown protested. "He told me she was losing her mind and it was for her health's sake."

Emily shook her head. "He drugged her so she would seem incompetent. He wanted to take control of her legacy. I've witnesses, too," Emily assured him. "If you're associated with this man, you must sever all ties with him immediately, lest he drag you down with him."

Emily could see him considering this; unconsciously Brown took a step away from the grave.

Pursuing her advantage, Emily added, "He also viciously attacked my sister."

"Miss Charlotte?" Brown asked in a small voice, as though this last piece of information were too much to bear. "What did he do?"

"Heaton hit her across the face with a riding crop." She embellished the story for effect. "She may bear the scar for life."

Almost under his breath, Brown said, "Little Miss Charlotte. She doesn't have any good looks to spare." He stared at the grave with revulsion, and Emily knew he was on their side.

In a voice loud enough for Heaton to hear, Brown said, "Those are serious charges, Miss Brontë." His son reappeared, carrying a ladder under his arm.

"Brown, I'll break you, too!" Heaton called up. "Don't you dare turn on me. I'm invoking the Mason's code."

"Shut up, Heaton," Brown snapped. Suddenly he seemed a different person, someone powerful and fearsome. He stalked over and stared down into the open grave. "I won't let your greed tarnish all the good work the lodge does. You have dishonored the fraternity. You'll be expelled at our next meeting."

"What should we do now?" Emily asked.

Brown ran his fingers through his thick fair hair. He turned to his son and told him to drop the ladder and fetch the constable. "Go as far as Bradford, if you have to."

Heaton's frantic voice called up. "Brown, don't listen to her! You have to help me!"

"Heaton, shut up," Brown said.

Emily called down, "My father will have Rachel seen by a doctor who will see she is perfectly sane, despite the laudanum you have dosed her with. And he'll bring you before a magistrate in Leeds. Someone you can't buy or threaten."

She turned to John Brown. "I'm sure my father will be out to speak to you in a moment. Good night, Mr. Brown."

She slipped away. At the parsonage gate she paused and looked back on the scene. She hoped to see her sisters Maria and Elizabeth, floating above the graveyard, enjoying the spectacle, but there were only markers for the dead, a confused sexton, and the voice of a very angry, frustrated, soon-to-be-former landowner and Freemason.

My help had been needed and claimed; I had given
it: I was pleased to have done something; trivial,
transitory though the deed was, it was yet an active
thing, and I was weary of an existence all passive.

CHAPTER TWENTY-SIX

Ten minutes earlier

After hearing Emily's hoots, Charlotte led the horse and cart carrying Rachel to one side of the house, then slipped in the gate and found the front door locked. She pounded on the door. Finally a worried Tabby answered.

"Miss Charlotte, where have you been?" Tabby cried. "Your father is frantic about you and your sister. And did you hear that terrible explosion? Your father thinks it was an earthquake!"

Keeper appeared in the hallway and bulled his way past them with a loud howl and disappeared into the garden.

"It wasn't an earthquake, it was a bog burst." Charlotte forestalled her questions. "I'll explain later, Tabby. Where is Father? There's a lady outside who needs our help."

Branwell appeared from the kitchen. "There you are! I told Tabby she was worrying for nothing."

"Mr. Branwell, you help bring in the poor lady; I'll make up a bed in the sitting room." Tabby bustled off, but not before saying, "Do I smell smoke?"

"What lady?" Branwell said. "Charlotte, you're soaking wet!" He looked closer. "What happened to your head?"

Charlotte didn't trust herself to speak. She led the way to the cart and lifted the horse blanket and showed Rachel to Branwell.

Branwell went pale. "That's Heaton's mad cousin."

"Sister," Charlotte corrected. "Heaton has been drugging her to make her seem mad. And you helped him."

"His sister? What are you talking about? It was a tonic prescribed by the doctor." He stepped back, shock on his face. "How do you know about that? Why is she here?"

"Because Emily and I rescued her from Robert Heaton." She fingered the dried blood on her forehead.

"You'll ruin everything!" Branwell started shouting in a high voice. "I've only just joined . . ." He gulped before continuing. "A new group of friends—who accept me."

Charlotte was impatient with his explanations and his secrets. "Branwell, Robert Heaton sponsored you to be a Freemason only to use you in his own schemes. He is not your friend."

"That's not true."

"It is," Charlotte said flatly. "Now help me bring Rachel inside."

"I don't dare go against Heaton." Branwell heard voices from the graveyard. "That's Heaton. He's here! Well, this makes it easier, Charlotte. If this woman is supposed to be here, he'll say so." He started to walk to the graveyard, hands cupping his mouth to amplify his shout. "Heaton!"

"Stop, Branwell!" Charlotte said. Something in her tone made him turn around. He saw what she was holding and blanched.

"Put that away!" he said.

Charlotte's hand was shaking as she pointed the pistol at Branwell. "Bring Rachel in. And don't cry out, or I'm liable to shoot something important. I've never had lessons like Emily."

※

Tabby fussed over a barely conscious Rachel on the couch. Branwell sat sulking at the table, glowering at Charlotte, who kept her hand on the pistol.

Rev. Brontë came in the room. He blinked when he saw Charlotte holding the pistol. "Charlotte, put that away. It's not a toy." He spied Rachel on the couch and rushed to bend down to her. "Who is this? Is she ill? Am I needed for the last rites?"

"Father," Charlotte implored, "please leave Mrs. Casson to us. Emily needs you in the graveyard."

Her father straightened up and gave Charlotte a sharp glance. "Mrs. Rachel Casson? Heaton's sister? Charlotte, what have you done?" Before she could answer, he noticed the cut on her face. "What happened?"

"Father, for heaven's sake! I am fine." She pointed to her bleeding head. "Robert Heaton did this to me. Emily drew him away so I could get this lady to safety. She needs our help. And Emily needs yours." She pulled the pistol out of her pocket. "Take this—you may need it. Go. Now!"

Blinking rapidly, Rev. Brontë seized the pistol and hurried outside.

"The poor thing," Tabby crooned, fussing over Rachel. "I'm going to get her a cold compress. You stay with her, Charlotte."

Glaring at her brother, Charlotte said, "I wouldn't think of leaving her alone, Tabby."

Charlotte went to the window and looked toward the graveyard. She could see her father's tall figure standing next to Emily and Keeper. Sexton Brown and his son were bringing a body out of an open grave. It was Robert Heaton! Chuckling, she reminded herself not to be surprised at anything if Emily was involved.

She returned to Rachel and checked she was still asleep. Branwell lifted his pale eyes to Charlotte and finally spoke. "Did Heaton really strike you?" he asked.

"Yes," she said simply.

"Why?"

"Does it matter?"

He put his head in his hands and ran his fingers through his thick red hair. "Of course not." His eyes filled with tears. "Was he really just using me?"

Charlotte hesitated, torn between punishing Branwell further and giving him comfort. She finally decided to do what Emily would do and tell the unvarnished truth.

"You were his pawn in his plot to cheat Rachel out of her father's inheritance. If Emily and I had not intervened, an innocent woman would have been committed to an asylum and robbed of her legacy. And you would have tarnished Father's life's work."

Branwell began to sob. Charlotte resisted her impulse to go to him. After a long moment of self-pity, he turned his head so he could look directly at her. "What will happen to me now?"

Charlotte was swept by a wave of complex feelings. Anger that Branwell's first thought was still of himself. But also ineffable sadness that the boy who had shown so much promise was reduced to this coward sniveling at the table. He stared at her, waiting for an answer. At last she said, "It depends on Rachel. Did you know what the tonic was for?"

"He told me she had nerves and suffered from delusions that people were trying to hurt her."

"No delusion," Charlotte said. "It was true. He was her enemy."

"Charlotte, you must believe me. I didn't know."

Charlotte wished she could believe him with a whole heart. "She might not press charges against you. And thanks to Emily and me, you never had a chance to alter Father's records."

"You know about that, too?"

"We know everything."

"But I didn't do it," Branwell said. He heaved a sigh of relief. "In fact, there's no proof I did anything at all."

At that moment, there was a fusillade of knocks at the door. They heard Emily's voice calling, "Open up!" The commands were interjected with deep barks from Keeper.

Tabby bustled down the hall to open the door, her pale complexion flushed. "Emily! First Charlotte comes in with that woman, drunk by the look of her! Then your father stormed outside with his pistol. Now you—covered with mud. What on earth is happening tonight?"

Branwell got up. "I can't face her, too," he said, and scurried up the stairs.

Without a word, Emily pushed past Tabby and went into the drawing room, not noticing Branwell's hasty departure.

"Emily!" Charlotte exclaimed, embracing her with wide-open arms. "Thank goodness you are safe. I sent Father to rescue you."

"I didn't need rescuing," Emily said. "However, Mr. Brown was badly in need of his guidance. Somehow Heaton fell into an open grave and broke his ankle."

Her hand to her mouth, Charlotte laughed, "What a shame!"

A wicked smile on her face, Emily said, "Yes, isn't it? He's in terrible pain."

Charlotte clapped her hands softly. "Well done, Emily!"

"I'm very tired now." Emily sank down on the stairs and closed her eyes. Charlotte sat down next to Emily and put an arm around her. With a grateful sigh, Emily lay her head on Charlotte's shoulder.

"Did you send a doctor to Harry?" Emily asked sleepily.

"Yes, it was the first thing I did once I got Rachel inside. Tabby sent the scullery maid to tell him to go directly to Top Withins," Charlotte said. "I only hope he's in time."

"As do I," Emily agreed.

After several moments of unprecedented unity between the sisters, Charlotte broke the silence. "Emily, what on earth happened to your petticoat?"

Emily's laughter echoed throughout the house.

You see, Mr. Lockwood, it was easy enough
to win Mrs. Heathcliff's heart.
But now, I'm glad you did not try.

EPILOGUE

Two weeks later

*E*mily's story poured from her fingers, filling page after page of foolscap paper. In her fictional world, the parsonage walls had dissolved and the north wind tossed her hair about, making her eyes water with its force.

Suddenly a loud knocking intruded as though a giant's fist had pounded the bog, bouncing her characters off their feet. Frantic, Emily grasped at the thread of her story, trying to pull herself back into the tale, but the pounding continued.

"Will someone answer the door?" she shouted. There was no response. Another knock. Muttering an oath, she shoved the papers away across the square dining room table and stalked to the front door. She pulled it open, ready to treat whoever had disturbed her writing with the disdain they deserved.

"Harry!" Her irritation dissolved. The loose bandages about his face and hands dismayed her, but she was glad to see his eyes were clear and lucid. "It's good to see you finally. Charlotte and I tried to visit you, but we were turned away every time."

"I'm sorry," he said. His voice was raspy as if from long disuse. "I wasn't ready for visitors, even if their name was Brontë."

She opened the door wide and stepped back, careful not to crowd him. How could she put him at ease? What would Charlotte do?

"Come in. You've never been to the parsonage before, have you? Here's the parlor. Won't you sit down while I get us some tea?" Her inconsequential talk of hospitality was foreign to their usual conversation, but she prattled on to give him time to find his footing.

When she returned with a tray from the kitchen, she half expected him to have fled. But he was standing by the fireplace, staring down at the carpet.

"This carpet has a very odd pattern of use," he said. "It's worn only on the edges."

Emily laughed, and the light sound seemed to put him further at ease. "In the winter, we sisters promenade around the room, arm in arm, reading from our stories or poems." She poured him a cup of tea. "Sugar or milk?"

"Two sugars, please," he said. "Your brother was never part of your writing?"

"Not since we were children. Now he writes in the privacy of his own room and refuses to share with us."

Harry's blue eyes darted around the room and glanced up the stairs. She understood what he hesitated to ask. "Branwell is gone. Father sent him off to Bradford to study painting. I think he'll remain there until after the trial."

"Trial." Harry pronounced the word with a finality that chilled the room.

Emily slowly stirred the sugar in the tea. "My father says your uncle is sure to be convicted of kidnapping, fraud, and injuring Charlotte. His Freemason friends have all deserted him, as have the other mill owners. He'll go to prison." She handed Harry the teacup, which he accepted with bandaged hands. She looked down at them for a long moment, then raised her eyes to his.

"The doctor says I'm lucky." Harry's voice was bitter. "I will regain full use of my fingers."

"That's good, isn't it?" Emily asked.

"Of course, but he can't say the same for my face." Before Emily could say anything, he put the cup down and unwound the bandages, his hands clumsy. The skin around his eyes was clear, but his cheeks to his chin were covered with raw patches of skin and unhealed blisters.

"Oh, Harry," Emily breathed. She reached toward him and he recoiled. Slowly, as though she were approaching one of her wild animals, Emily showed him she was only going to stroke his hair. He closed his eyes and let her hand soothe him. After a few moments, he pulled away slightly, but enough so that she knew to stop.

"I'm hideous," he whispered.

"Not to me," she said.

He shook his head and turned his back to her. She sipped her tea and waited for him to speak. Finally Harry said, "I'm here to say goodbye."

"Why?" Emily asked, staring down at the tea leaves floating in her cup.

"My mother has such terrible memories of Yorkshire, she wants to get well away," he explained. "I don't know if she can ever return to Ponden Hall."

"But . . ."

"It's done, Emily."

Emily blinked away an unexpected tear. "That's understandable, I suppose."

His clear eyes narrowed. "Really? Because I think you would confront your fears, not run from them."

"Perhaps," Emily said. "But then I'm not afraid of much."

"I know." With an echo of his old romantic bravado, Harry said, "You're extraordinary."

Emily stood up and began rearranging Aunt B.'s bric-à-brac on the mantel. Compliments always made her uncomfortable. She heard a noise in the hall, but didn't turn to look. Emily knew full well who was listening.

"I'm not so brave," Harry went on, oblivious to possible eavesdroppers. "I can't stand to see the pity on people's faces. Emily, when you greeted me at the door, you didn't look away. You're the first person to really look at me since the fire."

"In time . . ." Emily started to say.

"In time, the burns will heal. But my face will always be horrible."

"Not to me," Emily said again.

"I know, and I thank you for it." He looked at her for a long moment, as though trying to memorize every detail of her face. "If it weren't so presumptuous, I would love you for it."

Emily's hand jerked, and the tea sloshed out of her cup. She took out her handkerchief and mopped it up, taking a moment for them both to regain their composure. "That's a ridiculous reason to love someone."

"Can you give me a better reason?" he asked.

"Because you can't live without her."

He sighed. "Even before I was burned, you made it clear you could live without me."

"Harry . . ."

"Don't," he said. "I couldn't bear it if you lied to me. It would crush me if you pretended to love me only because I've been injured."

Slowly she said, "I would never do that."

A bark of laughter escaped his mouth, and if it was perilously close to a sob, neither of them made any reference to it.

"Where are you going?" Emily asked.

"I've rented a house in northern Scotland."

"That's very far," Emily replied.

"Far enough to discourage *any* visitors."

"I wish things were different," Emily said. She glanced down at her ink-stained fingers. "Perhaps if I were more traditional . . ."

"If you were the type of girl who wanted marriage and children and a household, you would not be my lovely, impetuous Emily." He caught her hands in his bandaged palms. "I'm so grateful for all your help," he said. "Without you and your sister, I would have nothing."

Emily stared at their hands, entwined together. After a few moments he released her.

"I'm glad I kissed you that day, Emily."

Emily smiled a crooked smile. "I believe I kissed *you*."

"So you did." He rewrapped his face with the bandages to protect the tender skin. "A memory I will cherish." He turned and walked away.

"Harry!" Emily said. He stopped. She ran to him and held out her arms. He hesitated and she stepped closer. Harry closed his eyes and let her embrace him. She held him gently for a long time.

Harry had tears in his eyes when he moved away. "Please give my regards to Charlotte."

"She will be sorry not to say goodbye to you in person."

"I don't want her to see me like this." He started for the door. "Farewell, Emily."

"Goodbye, dear Harry."

The echo of the front door closing hadn't faded before Charlotte walked into the parlor. Emily stood in the center of the room, staring into space. Charlotte, arms folded, waited until Emily noticed her presence.

"I hope you were able to hear everything from the hall," Emily said drily.

Charlotte didn't bother to deny it. "How can you let him go?"

Emily stared at her sister. "You heard him. He decided to leave." Her voice lacked her usual confidence.

"You could have changed his mind if you wanted to," Charlotte said. "But now that he's ugly, he's not good enough for you?"

Charlotte meant to be cruel, but Emily wondered if her sister was more right than she knew. Harry had not only lost his good looks but his confidence and bravado. Harry assumed he was no longer worthy of love, and the assumption almost made it true.

"You think I should have tried to convince him to stay?" Emily asked. "But I would never marry him. Or anyone for that matter."

"You are too cold," Charlotte said with conviction.

"I'm not cold," Emily cried. "I did care for him a little, but Harry deserves someone to love him with a whole heart." She glanced at the table with her pile of foolscap paper covered with her handwriting. "He would always have a rival for my affections."

"Writing is a poor substitute for love."

"Charlotte, I'm not in love with him! We had an adventure, but that doesn't mean I have to fall into his arms. I'm not some lovesick queen in one of your stories."

Charlotte recoiled as if she had been struck.

Emily winced. "I didn't mean it like that. I love your stories. But in real life, does the queen really want to live with the duke? If the queen ends up with the duke, what happens to her own kingdom?"

"I would give up my writing if I could have a great romance," Charlotte said. In a small, sad voice she added, "If he loved me, all the scars in the world would not keep me away from him."

"I don't think I'm destined for love," Emily said. "Even when it was most exciting with Harry, I was thinking all the time about how to tell the story on paper." She reached her hand out to Charlotte. "If you don't find love, you too can find solace in your stories."

Charlotte squeezed Emily's hand. "If I wrote this story, I'd choose a happier ending."

"I wouldn't," Emily assured her sister. "Life is full of tragedy, and so my stories will be, too."

Charlotte glared at her as long as she was able, then burst out laughing. "You're impossible! Must you disagree with me about everything?"

Emily nodded. "Probably." She returned to the table, picked up her pen, and began to write.

THE END

AUTHOR'S NOTE

𝒟ear Reader,

The more research I did about the Brontës, the more I marveled at the unlikelihood of three wonderful writers growing up in this tiny house on the edge of the lonely moors. Every member of the family was a fascinating character. Branwell, Anne, and Rev. Brontë could each be the main characters of their own novels, but I was most interested (and challenged) by trying to capture the complicated relationship between the two most famous Brontës: Charlotte and Emily. Emily was mesmerizing but also impossible to live with, while Charlotte tried so hard to be true to her artistic self while being the only practical person in a house full of brilliant lunatics.

The Brontë sisters lived a sheltered life in their father's parsonage overlooking a crowded graveyard. Theirs was the last house in town. They were equally isolated socially because there were no other middle-class families in Haworth. Beyond the parsonage lay the open moors, a wild and desolate place that shaped their world and their writing.

All the Brontë children died young, but during their short lives Charlotte, Emily, and even Anne (who is absent from *Always Emily*) wrote important novels that are considered classics today. Every few years a new movie or miniseries based on *Jane Eyre* or *Wuthering Heights* proves these books have not lost their attraction for modern readers.

Early death haunted the Brontës. Their mother died when the youngest child, Anne, was just a year old. The two oldest daughters, Maria (age eleven) and Elizabeth (age ten), contracted consumption (also known as the "graveyard cough"), or what we now call tuberculosis, at Cowan Bridge, a boarding school for poor clergymen's daughters. The conditions at the school were terrible; one third of the students died, causing a national scandal. Charlotte, who narrowly escaped illness at the school, was deeply affected by her time there. A thinly disguised version of Cowan Bridge became the model for Lowood, the cruel boarding school in Charlotte's famous novel *Jane Eyre*.

With the death of her older sisters, Charlotte abruptly became the oldest in the family, a position of responsibility she took quite seriously for the rest of her life. There's no proof that Emily and Charlotte snuck into the family crypt, but their sisters were taken from them so quickly that I wanted to give them an opportunity to say goodbye.

Not surprisingly, Rev. Brontë was reluctant to send his remaining children away to school again. Charlotte, Branwell, Emily, and Anne were schooled at home for the next several years. Their father gave them great freedom to read almost anything, so, unusually for the time period, the sisters read the same novels, history texts, and philosophical treatises as their brother.

The Brontë children were quick to take advantage of any library they could find, including the one at Ponden House, which was two miles from the parsonage. The children also liked to make up fantasy worlds and characters that inhabited them. By the time Charlotte was twelve, they were writing the stories down.

Charlotte and Branwell wrote about a fantasy kingdom called Angria, while Emily and Anne created Gondal. Charlotte in particular liked to bind her stories in tiny books that could fit in the palm of your hand. Her penmanship was excellent, but so small that a magnifying glass was required to read it. Recently one of these Brontë juvenilia (books written by children) sold at auction for nearly one million dollars.

Charlotte enrolled in the Roe Head School when she was sixteen. A diligent student, she excelled at her studies. Charlotte was always afraid of what would happen to her and her siblings if their father was to die. Not only was his salary the family's only income, but their home belonged to the church, too.

The options for young women to earn their own living were extremely limited in the 1830s, so not surprisingly Charlotte planned to become a teacher to support herself. After she finished her schooling, Charlotte was invited back to be a teacher at Roe Head. She was nineteen. Though she did not enjoy teaching, she stayed because part of her compensation included the cost of Emily's tuition.

At the age of seventeen, Emily was old to be a first-time student, and her time at Roe Head was not a success. Accustomed to complete freedom at home to read and write as she wished, as well as to take frequent treks on the moor in all weathers, she found life at school intolerable. She most likely missed her beloved pets. Besides her dogs Grasper and Keeper, she kept cats, geese, and even a pet hawk named Nero. Emily's homesickness became so debilitating that she went home after only a month to be replaced at school by her sister, Anne, a few months later.

In *Always Emily,* I sent Charlotte home from Roe Head just in time to help investigate the mystery. This visit home was fictional. However, I took the liberty of imagining what would have happened if the headmistress ever saw what Charlotte was writing. The story about the duke and the queen at the beginning of Chapter Two is my own invention, although typical of the high gothic romantic writing Charlotte favored as a teenager.

Anne, Charlotte, and Emily all tried their hand at teaching or being governesses, but none of their positions lasted for long. One of the few nonfamily members admitted into the Brontës' circle, Ellen Nussey, a school friend of Charlotte's, noted that she could not imagine any family whose temperament was less suited to teaching than the Brontës.

By 1846, all the Brontës had returned home. Charlotte finally abandoned the idea that the girls should earn their living by teaching.

One day Charlotte snuck a peek in Emily's portable desk and found a secret journal of her poetry. She remembered the experience of reading Emily's poems for the first time: "To my ear, they had a peculiar music—wild, melancholy, and elevating." Emily was furious with her sister's invasion of her privacy, but Charlotte thought the ends justified the means. The girls could support themselves with their writing. She convinced Anne and Emily to submit poems to a publisher.

In the 1840s, very few women published their work. The sisters knew that their writing would be judged unfairly simply because they were female, so they decided to submit it under pseudonyms that could be of either gender. Anne became Acton Bell, Charlotte was Currer Bell, and Emily took the name Ellis Bell.

Their poems were published and received favorable reviews. Unfortunately only two copies were sold. Charlotte then decided that the sisters should try writing novels, which were more lucrative.

Charlotte's first novel was rejected, but her second, *Jane Eyre,* was accepted and published. It tells the story of Jane, an impoverished and plain governess. After suffering as a child for the sins of being poor and outspoken, Jane becomes a governess for the enigmatic Mr. Rochester. Their tragic love story has become a classic, beloved by millions of readers.

It's hard for the modern reader to appreciate how Charlotte's novel defied conventions at the time. The novel is written in the first person, the first novel to feature a female protagonist speaking in her own intensely personal voice. And did she speak! Jane is honest about her passionate nature and the feelings she harbors for her employer. It was a shockingly original novel for its time.

Jane Eyre was an instant success. Some critics called it coarse because obviously women shouldn't have these sorts of feelings, and if they did, they certainly did not talk about them.

The identity of Currer Bell was the question of the day. The speculation intensified after the publication of equally unusual novels by Emily and Anne, also under their male pseudonyms.

Emily's only novel, *Wuthering Heights,* was published in 1847. A story of doomed love and revenge on the moors of Yorkshire, *Wuthering Heights* was often condemned as a brutal novel of amoral passion. However, now it is considered one of the most enduring pieces of writing in the English language.

Emily was supposed to have begun work on another novel, but became ill before she could finish it. She believed her health had been compromised by contamination of the parsonage's water from the church's graveyard. Despite her worsening condition, she refused to see a doctor. She died of tuberculosis in 1848 at the age of thirty. Upon her death, Keeper howled at her bedroom door all night, proving his loyal companionship even after death.

Unfortunately, Anne's novels have long been overshadowed by those of her more famous sisters. Her first novel, *Agnes Grey,* was based on her own experiences as a governess in a middle-class household. Her second, *The Tenant of Wildfell Hall,* about a woman who flees from an abusive husband, is considered one of the first truly feminist novels. Anne died of tuberculosis in 1849 at the age of twenty-nine, a year after Emily's death.

Despite his early promise, Branwell never succeeded in life. The only time he went away to school was in 1825, when he enrolled at the Royal Academy in London. He returned a week later, demoralized. His sisters never discovered what happened there.

Branwell drifted from one job to another. He drank and eventually became addicted to laudanum. He died at the age of thirty-two from tuberculosis, complicated by his addictions.

Some modern scholars have suggested that Branwell had an active role in writing his sisters' novels; however, the evidence for this is not convincing. In fact, Charlotte said that he didn't even know that his sisters had been published.

Charlotte was devastated by the deaths of her siblings. She would publish two more novels, *Shirley* and *Villette.* Although both were well received, neither received the acclaim that *Jane Eyre* had.

In 1854, she accepted a proposal of marriage from her father's assistant curate, Arthur Nichols. Her father initially opposed the match, perhaps because he feared losing his last remaining child. However, he finally agreed and the couple was married.

Charlotte became pregnant almost immediately. Unfortunately, she suffered from severe morning sickness, which aggravated her already poor health. She and her unborn child died in 1855. She was thirty-eight. Her official cause of death was tuberculosis, just like her siblings.

Any biography of the Brontë girls would not be complete without their father, who supported their thirst for knowledge and encouraged them to write. Rev. Brontë was a poor farmer's son in Ireland. He went to Cambridge on a scholarship and became an Anglican clergyman. His parish was in Haworth, a manufacturing town in the northeast of England, the setting for *Always Emily*. He brought his wife and six children to the parsonage in 1820.

After his wife's untimely death, his sister-in-law, Aunt Branwell, came to stay with them to help raise the children. For forty years, Tabitha Aykroyd was the family's housekeeper. The children spent many hours in the kitchen listening to her gossip about the parish. The character of Ellen, the talkative and loving servant, in *Wuthering Heights* is assumed to be based on Tabby.

Rev. Brontë was a brilliant and fiery preacher who scrupulously cared for the members of his large parish. He was a political figure who openly opposed the mill owners who mistreated their employees. He feared for his safety and carried a pistol when he was out in the parish. His habit of firing the pistol every morning that I wrote about was well-documented. The pistol could only be unloaded by firing it.

He was famous for his punctuality and his prodigious memory. He feuded frequently with the laundrywomen in town, who insisted on draping their wet sheets over the tombstones to dry. I couldn't resist using this detail in the final confrontation between Emily and Robert Heaton in the graveyard. Cataracts nearly blinded the reverend until 1847, when he had an operation to remove them (using a hand-cranked drill!) that enabled him to regain his sight. Rev. Brontë survived all of his children.

Many details from the lives of the Brontës inspired events in this novel.

Top Withins is a remote and lonely house that many consider to be Emily's inspiration for *Wuthering Heights*. The Heatons were a family who lived nearby in Ponden House. Ponden House is widely considered to be the basis of Thrushcross Grange, a house in *Wuthering Heights*.

My favorite scene in *Wuthering Heights* is when Cathy and Heathcliff are outside, staring into the luxurious library at the Grange. I deliberately recalled that moment when Emily and Harry look into the well-lit library at Ponden House.

It was rumored that a daughter of the Heaton family made an imprudent marriage and had a sickly son who would have been a contemporary of the Brontë sisters. Another Heaton family story tells of an exiled son of the house coming back to take his revenge on other members of the family who had wronged him. I combined the two stories to invent my fictional Harry's quest to find his mother, Rachel.

The bog burst that occurs when Emily and Charlotte are racing back to the parsonage is based on an event that happened in 1824. While the children were out on the moors, a seven-foot-high mudslide swept across the moor, taking out bridges, ruining fields, and poisoning the water table.

The Freemasons are not nearly as sinister as I made them appear. The group has existed since the late sixteenth century and today claims six million members. While the Masons do have secret rituals, their main purposes are charitable works, living by high moral standards, and the fostering of fraternal friendship. Branwell did join the Freemasons for a time under the tutelage of the Worshipful Master, Sexton John Brown. The Three Graces Lodge was on Newall Street, which is now called Mason Street.

Emily did, in fact, cauterize her own arm to prevent hydrophobia, or rabies, after a dog bite. Charlotte used the detail in her novel, *Shirley,* written after Emily's death.

Despite having the benefit of reading the biography and their work together, I often couldn't decide which Brontë sister was my favorite. Only Emily could have written Cathy and Heathcliff's story in *Wuthering Heights,* and only Charlotte could have given a voice to *Jane Eyre.* In *Always Emily,* Emily owns the mystery that takes place on the moors, and the chance of romance is hers. But Charlotte, despite fighting her own demons, manages to rescue a stranger and her beloved brother.

In the end, I leave the choice of favorite Brontë sister to you, the reader. And if you haven't read their books . . . what are you waiting for?

QUOTE ATTRIBUTIONS

May 1825—introductory segment
    From *Wuthering Heights* by Emily Brontë
Chapter Oné
    From *Jane Eyre* by Charlotte Brontë
Chapter Two
    From a private letter by Charlotte Brontë
Chapter Three
    From a private letter by Charlotte Brontë
Chapter Four
    From *Wuthering Heights* by Emily Brontë

ACKNOWLEDGMENTS

*W*riting is a lonely profession unless you are lucky enough to have a critique group like mine. Sari Bodi, Christine Pakkala, and Karen Swanson are my harshest critics and most vocal supporters. Incidentally, they are my closest friends.

My editor, Victoria Rock at Chronicle Books, has always championed my work and supported my creative decisions (except when I had gone a little astray . . .). The team at Chronicle makes it easy to write, especially Taylor Norman and Lara Starr. I owe the gorgeous cover to Kate Cunningham and the clever art direction to Sara Gillingham.

My agent, George Nicholson, and his assistant, Caitlin McDonald, at Sterling Lord Literistic always offer encouragement and even more importantly explanations of those long contracts. They worry about stuff so I don't have to.

In the middle of the long process between idea and final draft, I was able to attend the Stone Spirit Farm Work in Progress Retreat. Five days later I had a clear plan to substantially revise my novel, and twenty new friends. I'd particularly like to thank Tanya Lee Stone and Laurie Halse Anderson, who convinced me that the Brontë sisters would applaud any historical liberties if it served my story. As Laurie said, "The back matter is your friend." My group included Cheryl Bardoe, Leslie Cahill, and Sarah Goff. Their advice was thoughtful, useful, and generous.

Finally, I have to acknowledge my debt to my teenaged daughters, Margaux and Rowan. *Always Emily* is at its heart a story about brilliant sisters who could not be more different from each other. I only have to watch my children to see the same dynamic play out, day after day. Someday I hope they will learn to appreciate each other—just as Emily and Charlotte finally did.

Always Emily
DISCUSSION GUIDE

- At the start of *Always Emily*, we see the Brontë children at the funeral of their sister, Elizabeth. How does their behavior during this difficult time help create an understanding of the personalities of each of the surviving siblings? Does this behavior remain consistent throughout the rest of the novel?

- Though they are sisters, Emily and Charlotte Brontë have quite distinctive personalities. How are they similar to each other? How are they different? Are they the type of people you'd want to have as friends? Why or why not?

- How would you characterize the relationship between Emily and Charlotte? Do you feel that it changes over the course of the novel? If so, in what ways?

- Though her family fears for her safety when Emily takes solitary walks on the moors, the moors are the place where Emily seems happiest. What is it about this landscape that speaks to Emily? In what ways does it inspire her writing?

- Consider the quotes from the Brontë sisters' own writing that are used to introduce the chapters. How do their words help set the tone for the story? Did you have a particular favorite or one you enjoyed most?

- As their father is a clergyman, the Brontë family lives in the church's parsonage. What are the advantages and disadvantages of living in property owned by the church? How would you feel about living in close proximity to a graveyard?

- When Miss Wooler questions Charlotte about her father's position regarding the business practices of mill owners, Charlotte states, "My father tells the truth even when it's not to his benefit. He's very brave." Consider Charlotte's position about her father. Do you agree with her opinion? What would you do if you were in his situation?

- Why do Emily and Charlotte feel so determined to solve the mystery of Mr. Heaton and his sister? Do you think the danger they put themselves in is justified? Why or why not?

- How would you describe Branwell? Is he a likeable character? Why or why not?

- At the end of the story, Emily chooses not to pursue a relationship with Harry. If you were Emily, what would you have done?

A Sneak Peek at a NEW novel from Michaela MacColl

Available wherever books are sold.
For more distinctive books for teens, visit chroniclebooks.com/teen.

CHAPTER ONE

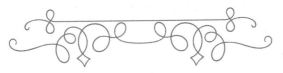

"Don't you wish we had the money papa
lost when we were little, Jo?
Dear me! How happy and good we'd be,
if we had no worries!"

*Y*ou're leaving me?"

Her father's words floated through the cracks in the door.

Louisa stifled a cry. Marmee would never leave them. Through all their suffering, the one constant was that the family must and would stay together.

Abandoning her desk, Louisa pressed her ear to the door that led to the parlor. She strained to hear her mother's answer.

"Bronson, you've left me no choice." Marmee's voice was tight, as though her vocal cords had been wrung like a wet rag.

Louisa opened the door with one finger, just a bit, to see her mother pacing back and forth across the narrow parlor. With a ripple of shock, Louisa noticed that Marmee's dark gray-streaked hair had come loose from her bun. Louisa stroked one of her own untidy braids in solidarity.

"I can't economize any more," Marmee said. "We've used up our credit in every shop in Concord. We can't afford to stay in this house or buy necessaries for the children." Her voice grew stronger, then faded as she paced away from the door. "If you won't work for money, I shall have to. It's a good job. They want me to run the hotel and manage the water cures."

Craning her neck, Louisa could just make out her father's face, as handsome and stubborn as ever. But his voice shook as he said, "It's so far. Waterford is a hundred and fifty miles away. What if the children need you?" Father was reclining on the comfortable sofa, his hands interlaced behind his gray-streaked blond head, his long legs stretched out in front of him. But his indifference was a pose; he would be lost without Marmee. They all would be.

"What the children need is to go to school," Marmee said. "But we can't afford it."

"Bah! What better teachers could they have besides me, Emerson, and Thoreau?" he asked with his usual confidence.

"Millionaires would pay a fortune for their children to have such an education."

"But their education, such as it is, lacks method and discipline."

"All the better!" Bronson exclaimed. "You know my methods. Our children thrive without the confines of a schoolroom and a harsh schoolmaster."

"Anna is only seventeen and she has to work for her living far from home. And what about Louisa? She should be going to parties and enjoying herself, as I did when I was her age." Poor Marmee—her voice was so tired and discouraged.

"When I was their age I was working on the farm," Bronson argued.

"But I enjoyed Boston's finest society, going to the theater and to parties. I want the girls to have some fun in their lives."

Huddled against the door, Louisa slid down to the floor and sighed. She definitely would prefer the theater to working for a living. Louisa knew she should find a job like Anna had, but she hated teaching and sewing and all the respectable ways she could earn money. And anything that pulled her away from writing her stories and poems was a waste of her time.

"A little sacrifice is good for them," Bronson said. "Our daughters must seek fields of richer thyme than we grow here. Let each of them make honey for herself, since all lasting enjoyments come from one's own exertions." Louisa heard him get up and rummage about the small desk in the parlor.

Louisa pushed open the door a little further. Her father was writing in one of his leather-bound journals. "That bit about bees is quite good," he muttered. "I might work that into one of my Conversations."

Marmee stood, her profile to Louisa, watching him write. The line of her back was rigid, and her hands were clenched. "You haven't had a paying Conversation in months, Bronson," Marmee said hotly. Then with a deliberate calming breath, Marmee moved close to her husband and placed her work-worn hands on his shoulders. "Come with me!" she murmured in his ear. "The hotel would like you to come and teach classes. They think you would be a great attraction." Her voice became husky. "You'd be supporting the family, and we could be together."

"Ah," breathed Louisa. So this was Marmee's plan.

Her parents had moved to a part of the room where she couldn't see them. Just as she moved to nudge the door open, she heard footsteps, light but firm, crossing the floor. She pulled back. The door closed with a decisive click.

She pressed her ear against the door, straining to hear her father's response to Marmee's entreaty.

"My dear, my work is in my mind and in the hard labor I do to grow our food and fix our house." Father's voice was only slightly muffled by the oak door. "I have no calling to work for others. Do not ask me to compromise my principles for money!"

"You would have us starve for your principles instead?" Even without seeing them, Louisa could tell her mother was close to tears.

Her father's voice took on a wheedling sound that put Louisa's teeth on edge. "Abba, you used to be proud of my ideas and principles. But you've changed, grown cold and unsympathetic. Now you complain like the most common housewife that there isn't enough money for fripperies."

Louisa glanced up at the few dresses hanging in her narrow closet. Each one was a hand-me-down from some rich relation, turned out and resewn to make a serviceable gown. Fripperies? She'd gladly settle for a fresh bolt of calico.

"Fripperies? Bronson, there isn't any money to pay for firewood. Or flour. Or your precious journals."

"Your family . . ."

"My family's generosity has been exhausted time and time again. Even my brother, who admires you greatly, wonders why you will gladly take the money that others have worked for, but you won't work yourself."

Louisa had only the vaguest memories of her father ever working for his living. When she was three, he had a school in Boston. His revolutionary ideas included fresh air in the classroom, no corporal punishment, and the strange idea that children could also teach the teachers. At first wealthy parents had flocked to the school but Bronson's other ideas had frightened them away. Almost sixteen now, Louisa couldn't recall her father working for money any time since, no matter how bare the larder. Father's willingness to let the family suffer for his ideals had been proven beyond a scintilla of doubt.

Marmee went on, ice in her voice. "I've been offered a contract for three months and you give me no choice but to take it."

"But who will take care of me?" Bronson asked indignantly.

Louisa pressed her forehead against the doorjamb, steeling herself against the answer.

"Louisa will," Marmee said. "She's a fine housekeeper."

Louisa scrambled to her feet and burst into the room. "Marmee! You can't leave me here to do everything! Beth's no help—she's still recovering from her winter cold. And baby May won't do anything but draw. You expect me to do all the cooking and the cleaning and the shopping and take care of them, too? I'll never have the chance to write." She was running out of breath, so she made sure to finish with a flourish. "It's not fair that just because Father won't get a job I have to be a slave!"

"Louisa!" Both Marmee and Bronson cried at once.

"A young lady never stoops to eavesdropping," Marmee said in a forbidding voice.

"Honest labor to care for your family is not slavery!" Bronson scolded as his wife took a breath. "You've met true slaves. You know the cruelty they suffer. By comparing yourself to a slave, you demean both you and them."

Louisa closed her eyes and pressed her fists against her eyelids. "I'm sorry," she whispered.

"Go back to your room," Marmee said. "And quietly. There's no need to wake your sisters. We'll talk later."

Her eyes averted from her parents, Louisa slowly crossed the parlor to her room, closing her door behind her. When they had bought Hillside House a few years ago, the house had been too small for Father, Mother, and four Alcott daughters, not to mention all the constant visitors. So her inventive father had cut an old workshop on the property in two and grafted each half onto opposite sides of the house. Louisa's tiny room, the first she had ever had to call her own, was in one half of the repurposed building, with a second door that opened directly into the garden.

Louisa shoved her bare feet into her boots, jerked her shawl from its hook, and slipped into the garden. Her ability to sneak out at night was her private antidote to the press of so many people. The chilled night air stung her skin and a breeze stirred her nightdress about her knees. Perched on a bench her father had fashioned from an old log, she brought her knees up to her chin.

Marmee couldn't leave them. Father could and did, traveling often to talk to other philosophers. But Marmee was their rock. Their shield against poverty and despair. Their financial situation must be even worse than Louisa knew for Marmee to consider leaving. But Louisa had only been thinking of how it affected her. She was ashamed of her own selfishness.

Money. Money. Money. How she hated being dependent on the kindness of friends and family. Louisa was tired of being grateful. She had looked for a job in Concord but there were none to be had. It was a pretty place, but dull. The townspeople thought the Alcotts were wild and strange. It was only because of Mr. Emerson that they had moved there. If it weren't for him and Mr. Thoreau, Concord would indeed be the "cold, heartless, brainless, soulless Concord" Marmee called it. But even Mr. Emerson couldn't conjure up work so Louisa could contribute to the family's finances.

The house faced busy Lexington Road, although it was mostly quiet at this hour. From the corner of her eye, Louisa caught a glimpse of movement in the shrubs by the front windows. She retreated to her door and reached for the stout walking stick she kept there.

"Who's there?" she called, forcing a quaver down.

A cracking noise of a foot on a twig, then a deliberate silence.

"I said, who is there?" Holding the walking stick up in front of her face, she stepped forward and peered around the corner. Next to the parlor's big bay window there was a dark figure, barely visible against the olive color of the house. Suddenly, the figure blinked, revealing the frightened whites of his eyes. She realized that his darkness was not the cover of night but the color of his skin.

"What's your business here?" she asked, her voice stern.

"Excuse me, Miss." The man's voice was deep and hesitant. "Are you the Stationmaster?"

Louisa sighed. Exactly what the Alcott family needed right now. Another fugitive slave.

MICHAELA MACCOLL

studied multidisciplinary history at Vassar College and Yale University, which turns out to be the perfect degree for writing historical fiction. This is her fourth novel. To learn more about Michaela and her work, please visit www.michaelamaccoll.com.

OTHER NOVELS OF INTRIGUE & ROMANCE BY MICHAELA MACCOLL:

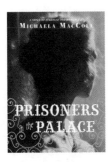

To learn more visit www.chroniclebooks.com/michaelamaccoll.com.